DESTINY DENIED

ROSEMARY GARD

This book is written for my grandsons:

Kevin Browne
Rory Browne
Thomas Browne

And, as always, is dedicated to the memory of Janice Thrall,
a true patroness of the arts.

"Every man has his own destiny: The only imperative is to follow it, to accept it, no matter where it leads him."

--Henry Miller

PROLOGUE

STEFAN'S JOURNEY...1907

Stefan had to leave. His distraught mother was talking about killing anyone who would try to take away what she felt rightfully belonged to her son. His Teta Sofie adopted the peasant Katya as her own daughter, meaning there was the possibility that Stefan was no longer his aunt's heir. And now it was publicly known that Ivan Balaban was not the blacksmith's son, but really Stefan's half brother. Would Ivan now be an heir to the Vladeslav holdings?

And...there was the terrifying Turk wanting more money for a gambling debt. Stefan had to leave!

No one at the house saw Stefan leave. Leading his horse through the thick forest on the hilltop road, he followed the narrow path. Watching the Gypsy camp on the hill, near the road was Ivan, seated looking down. Neither spoke when Ivan turned to look up at Stefan, each of them knowing they had to part.

When handsome Stefan reached Zagreb, he sold his horse and saddle to buy a ticket on the Orient Express which was headed for Istanbul, at that time known as Constantinople.

The Orient Express consisted of two baggage cars, four sleeping coaches, each with up to sixteen beds, and a restaurant coach.

Stefan's personal steward had the good manners not to look disapprovingly at the small bag Stefan handed him. The steward escorted Stefan to compartment twelve. The cabin was a very nice sitting room with a mirror, comfortable settee and a table. The cabin could easily be converted into a sleeping room at night. The W.C. or bathroom was at the end of the rail car. The cabin doors opened out onto a narrow, window-lined corridor with low benches available for seating. At night, the steward in charge of the cabins in his rail car slept on the comfortable benches, always on call, ready to serve.

"Pull this cord if you wish tea or anything else." The thin balding steward named Marian, said. He wore a crisp grey uniform with bright brass buttons. He showed Stefan the thick grey cord to pull for service. Before leaving, Marian asked, "Is there anything Monsieur needs? You will be notified when meals are being served."

Marian opened the door to leave, taking another look around to see that he had not overlooked anything. Through the open door an elderly woman, perhaps a governess, dressed in grey, paused to stare at Stefan. The white-haired woman moved on as Marian backed out of the door, closing it.

Removing his gloves, Stefan looked around. This was very elegant…perhaps too elegant. He was out of money. This may have been a foolish plan. Actually, it hadn't been a plan. He saw the train at the station and boarding it was a spur of the moment decision. What if he doesn't meet a rich woman who needs a companion for the summer? He was used to having women pay for his companionship in Zagreb, but on the Orient Express it may be another matter.

*The meals…*he didn't think to ask if the meals were included in his ticket. What was he going to do when it was time to go to the restaurant car and a bill might be presented? It was now even more obvious to him that he had not properly thought out abandoning his home in Vladezemla. Was he expected to dress for dinner? His wardrobe was lacking the essentials for such company as he might meet on this train. The Orient Express was the equivalent of a luxury hotel on wheels. How long could he go without eating, he wondered? Could he stay in his compartment during the whole trip?

He was so deep in thought, that the gentle knock at the door startled him.

"Yes, come in." he said.

Marian, the steward, handed Stefan a note. Stefan read it.

"Does Monsieur wish to send a reply?" the steward asked.

"No…no, that won't be necessary."

Stefan smoothed his hair and looked at this handsome reflection in the small mirror on the back of the door. His dark hair framed a face with the smooth complexion any woman would envy. He had nice straight teeth, not something so common in the early 1900's. He liked what he saw and winked at his reflection with those blue eyes, the eyes that made most women melt.

He straightened his cravat and brushed the lint from his blue coat. He was being summoned by a woman. Was she the daughter of a wealthy American businessman? He could say he was the son of a count or even introduce himself as a count. Rich Americans were impressed by royalty. Oh, if he had only brought more clothes!

The note read: "Please join me in #16 for dinner." It was signed, "A lady friend."

As he left his number twelve compartment on the short trip to compartment sixteen, he hoped this lady friend was a beauty. He was in no position to be choosy. It didn't matter what she looked like, just as long as she needed a paid companion for the summer, or longer if she wished.

At the door of compartment sixteen, Stefan smoothed his hair once more and straightened his cravat before gently knocking.

The door was opened by the same white-haired woman dressed in a grey long skirt and grey jacket, who had stared at him through the open door of his compartment. The woman stepped aside to let Stefan enter. He assumed her to be a servant. The lady friend who sent the note was probably inside, thought Stefan as he looked around. The woman closed the door and with hands on her hips, threw her head back laughing heartily.

Thinking this was some sort of a trick, or perhaps a trap, Stefan instinctively reached for the door handle ready to leave.

"This is too wonderful," said the prim older woman, no longer laughing, but smiling broadly. "I can't believe Stefan Vladeslav will be my traveling companion." She motioned for him to be seated. "We have so much to talk about."

When he hesitated, she said, "Please, please make yourself comfortable."

Seated in a comfortable velvet backed chair, still bewildered, Stefan studied the woman warily. He said nothing, just stroked his chin. The voice…he was sure he had heard that voice before. But, he could not place this prim matron standing before him. Had she been a governess? No…none of his friends had been cared for by a governess. After a few moments he said, "Forgive me, it appears you know me, but I must apologize, I cannot place you."

"I am hurt." She pretended to be offended. "You don't remember those nights when I greeted you at my door and let you gamble even when you had no money…shame on you." She playfully admonished.

With a look of wonder, Stefan rose from the chair and studied the woman's smiling face. He looked deep into her small eyes, the color no longer the bright blue of her youth, but now a pale hue. Her face was fleshy. Her hands looked so familiar. He stepped back and looked at her. Her white hair was coiled on top of her head. A ruffled collar surrounded her lined throat. He envisioned her with hennaed hair, her eyes outlined with kohl and her cheeks colored with rouge. He recalled seeing her wearing a bright orange caftan, standing at the entrance of the gambling house on that terrible night…the night he first met the Turk!

Stefan didn't say anything for a long time. Still not sure, hesitantly he said, "Magda, can it be you?"

Now her face crinkled with joy and she threw her arms around him. "Oh, Stefan, I never thought I would see you alive again."

Seeing his perplexed look, she added, "Abuh said he would kill you if you did not pay him the money he wanted. So," she added, "you must have paid him."

"I never saw him." Stefan was surprised. "When did he say he would kill me?

"The same night I decided to leave." she said. "He was on his way to see you."

Stefan remembered the awful Turk and his arrogant sneer. A round man, dressed in black pants, black vest, with a red fez atop his head. Stefan didn't want to think about the Turk…the frightening Turk.

Still holding her hand he asked, "What is this? Why the drastic change in appearance? Have you taken a position as a governess or nanny?"

She waived her plump hand at the chair. "Sit down."

With a firm pull of a cord she summoned the cabin steward.

"Let's have dinner here together." she said. "We have so much to talk about."

When Marian arrived, Magda asked, "Is the compartment next to mine occupied?"

The steward's discreet eyes glanced briefly at Stefan, "No, Madam, it is available."

"Good, then have my nephew's things moved there and unlock the adjoining door."

"Yes, Madam," said Marian a bit smugly, assuming Stefan to be a gigolo.

"Mama will be surprised when I tell her I ran into Teta Magda on the train." This was said loud enough by Stefan for Marian to hear. It didn't matter, for the steward didn't care what went on, as long as he was remembered with a good tip at the end of the journey. Marian had witnessed many romantic encounters on the Orient Express, all of them far more interesting and romantic than this encounter of what he thought to be an old nanny and a young gigolo.

Magda said to the steward, "We will have some tea now and our dinner in the cabin this evening."

"Yes, Madam," Marian bowed as he exited, but not without giving Stefan a long look.

At dinner, tasting the spicy soup Stefan said, "So you have run away from the Turk."

"And you have run away from your family," replied Magda, adjusting the linen napkin on her lap.

Magda listened as Stefan told her about Katya, of Ivan being his half brother and his Mother's obsession with the family money. It seemed so natural for him to unburden himself to her. It was indeed as if she were his real Teta, his aunt.

They were very comfortable with each other and discussed many private and personal things during the delicious meal. Wine was served with dinner and it made them more relaxed. With dinner completed, Marian removed the plates and brought in coffee and brandy, leaving a dessert tray.

With her feet comfortably on a foot stool, Magda sipped her coffee. She looked at Stefan, cup in one hand, her cigarette in the other and marveled at how handsome he was. They smoked and sipped in contented silence. After a while, Magda said, "We must decide what we are going to do. I have some money, but not enough to last us if we want to live comfortably."

Stefan gave Magda a long look. *What did she have in mind?*

"We?" he asked. "Are we to be a couple?"

Stefan didn't expect her wild burst of laughter. "Stefan! Look at me," she demanded, "I am not a young woman. What did you think I meant?"

His face reddened. He was embarrassed that he mistook her meaning.

Before he could say anything, Magda went on, "We could travel together with you as my devoted nephew and I your aunt." When he didn't respond, she continued, "We will stay at the finest hotels. We shall get some very fashionable and expensive clothes while we travel about Italy and France gambling."

Stefan straightened in his chair, his eyes grew wide. He liked the idea.

"What if we lose all your money?" He asked.

"We won't." She pointed a finger at him. "You will play and I will watch." She added, "I may play occasionally, when it is socially acceptable."

Magda could see him thinking this over. She said, "I can spot a cheater easily and I can predict who has the winning hand or who is bluffing. I have watched card players for many years and learned to read their faces and actions."

"But, how will you let me know?" He was interested in this plan.

"We will work out a series of signals. For instance, if I fool with my right earring, it could mean one thing, while using my fan could mean something else."

They talked long into the night working out the signals and decided to get off the train at the next stop to head back towards Italy. When it was time for Stefan to go to his adjoining compartment, he politely kissed Magda's hand. Gone was the tinted red haired woman who owned Magda's and gone was the irresponsible young man. They would carry themselves in a manner suggesting a wealthy aunt traveling with her nephew.

In time that was what they became. Stefan was respectful of Magda and she treated him like a loving family member, never overstepping herself or making demands. After all, she understood men better than most mothers and wives did. When he needed romantic company, she appeared not to notice.

Madame Magda Petrovich and her nephew, Stefan Vladeslav arrived at the lovely Grand Hotel Gardone, in Brescia Italy on the shore of Lago di Garda.

"Contessa Petrovich," announced Antonio, the pleasant manager of the hotel, bowing low. "We have an excellent suite of rooms for you and the Count with a magnificent view of the lake." He turned and gave Stefan a courteous bow.

Magda bestowed a gracious smile on the stocky manager and offered her hand, which he politely lifted to his lips.

Such a grand lady! *True nobility*, thought Antonio, as he waved to the uniformed porters to hurry with the trunks and cases.

Everyone loved Contessa Petrovich. She and her nephew never displayed superior attitudes, but were always so gracious and charming.

The elegant Hotel Gardone had been built in 1884 and offered all the richness the late Victorian Era had to offer. The oriental carpets along with comfortable brocade sofas and chairs were symbols of elegance and comfort for their elite guests. Crystal chandeliers sparkled in the sunlight and in the evening, when lit, reflected on the etched glass doors leading to the superb restaurant.

Magda, the former owner of a gambling house and brothel, along with Stefan, the disappointing son of Anton Vladeslav, never alluded to the titles of Countessa and Count. The fine clothes they wore, the elegant manner in which they spoke and conducted themselves, led people to assume they were nobility.

"Magda Petrovich," she would say when meeting someone new, extending her hand in greeting, "and my nephew, Stefan Vladeslav."

They were polite to the staff, never demanding or condescending. Sometimes Magda would present the hotel manager, with a cravat or stick pin as a gift, ensuring the finest attention should they visit that hotel again.

It took only six months of traveling throughout Italy and France, always staying in the best hotels, for Magda and Stefan to become, in a manner of speaking, celebrities.

"We have the same rooms that you occupied on your last stay with us." said Antonio watching Magda closely for a hint of disapproval should something be out of place or displeasing to her.

"It is beautiful as always, Antonio." Magda made a point of remembering names and using them whenever appropriate. "And the flowers are lovely." She lifted her hand to indicate the colorful floral arrangements which stood on almost every table.

"It is an honor that you wish to stay with us. I have engaged Amelia as your maid during your stay. She took care of you the last time you were here."

Magda nodded approvingly, "Thank you, I like Amelia."

"What about Santino?" Stefan asked about the slender valet he remembered from a previous stay. "Is he available?"

"Ah, yes!" Antonio beamed with pleasure that his cousin Santino was requested. "He is already in your room attending to your clothes."

Magda turned to the windows taking in the scenic view of beautiful Lake Garda. The long slim lake stretching from north to south had been a luxury summer destination even for the ancient Romans.

"Can I do anything more for you, Madam?" asked Antonio, "Also, refreshments are on the way." he added.

Magda looked at Stefan, who was seated on a blue and white brocade chair. "Anything you need?"

"No, Teta, everything is perfect as always." Stefan said Teta whenever he could to ensure the notion that they were aunt and nephew.

Antonio smiled, seeing everything in order he was about to leave when Magda asked, "Have arrangements been made for our evening's entertainment?"

"Ah, yes, Contessa. Signor Anello has extended an invitation to his villa. He asked me to say that you will know everyone attending and that it will be the usual sort of gathering."

As if considering the invitation, Magda asked Stefan, "Do you feel like a game of cards tonight?"

Stefan rose from the chair. "Yes, let's go. Salvatore is such a gracious host and his friends are pleasant."

"Molto buono, very good," said Antonio. "Signor Anello will send a carriage for you at eight, if that is convenient for you."

With Amelia, in Magda's room, unpacking the trunks and Santino in Stefan's room doing the same, Magda and Stefan were careful not to discuss their business or be overheard.

"Let's go on the terrace." said Magda opening the tall glass door leading to the sunny balcony. A warm breeze scented by lemon trees, flowers and the lake greeted them.

"This may be our last trip to Salvatore's." said Magda. "He makes me uncomfortable."

"How is that?" asked Stefan, lighting a cigarette, scanning the beach below for beautiful sun bathers.

She thought of Salvatore for a moment. He was a big man, salt and pepper hair and beard, "His eyes…," she replied, "he watches us too closely."

Everything is determined, the beginning as well as the end, by forces over which we have no control. It is determined for the insect, as well as for the star. Human beings, vegetables, or cosmic dust, we all dance to a mysterious tune, intoned in the distance by an invisible piper.

--**Albert Einstein**

CHAPTER 1

Spring 1909 – Croatia

The enjoyment of traveling and gambling was not the same without Magda. She had died in the city of Vicenza, near Venice. Her lingering cold developed into pneumonia. Stefan saw to it that she had a Catholic burial and her grave had a stone marker. She had been his best friend and another mother to him.

After two years of traveling, he was coming home...home to Vladezemla.

Surely his mother, Ernesta, had long ago forgiven him for taking her precious earrings as payment for his gambling debt to the Turk. The earrings were given to Ernesta by her mother on the day of her wedding to Stefan's father.

Stefan Vladeslav, riding in a hired carriage, surveyed the lush green countryside of his family's land. It appeared that nothing had changed during the time he had been away. The earth, the budding trees and the livestock smells were as he remembered. It was a beautiful day.

He saw the Gypsies camped on Marko Balaban's land just as they had been on the day he left, two years ago. Smoke from campfires rose like sentinels curling toward the sky. Beautiful dark women in colorful blouses and men with suspicious, watchful eyes went about their daily tasks. The painted caravans dotted the field and the Gypsy children played chasing one another as all children do. Every year the Gypsies came at the same time, thru Vladezemla in Croatia, pausing to rest, having a festival of sorts and doing some trading while on their way to France for their annual pilgrimage to Saint Maries de la Mer.

The clip clop of the horse's hooves and the gentle swaying of the carriage relaxed Stefan.

In the distance he saw the familiar sight of barefoot children herding cows and sheep grazing in the far, high green fields. Several women were at the river washing their clothes, beating them on rocks then draping the laundry on bushes to dry.

A babushka wearing peasant woman, dressed in a long cream colored homespun skirt, walked past the carriage. Balanced on her head was a large basket full of soiled clothing. She nodded respectfully at Stefan. She should have recognized him, but didn't. His black hair wanted to curl, but he now kept it combed straight back with the aid of pomade. His eyes were as blue as ever and still mesmerized women who dared look deep into them. A well trimmed mustache made him more handsome and he appeared older than his 22 years. He was dressed in the continental manner wearing a dark grey suit, a white ruffled shirt and a maroon cravat. Next to the soft Italian leather shoes he wore, rested a carpet bag, while a trunk and a leather case were tied to the back of the carriage.

Stefan could see the entrance to his family home with the fence made of stacked field stones and beyond the entrance was the large house where he grew up. The land was called Vladezemla, meaning the land of Vladeslav. The land had been an award from a King to an ancestor of Stefan's for leading a victorious ancient battle.

Stefan laughed out loud when he saw what was atop the house's chimney. There he saw a stork settling on a nest. How pleased his mother must be, he thought. She always said that a stork nest on the chimney meant good luck.

Teta Sofie would be happy to see him, he thought. His father's sister always forgave him when he fibbed or was rude. He knew his old maid aunt loved him. That would never change. She would forgive him for being gone so long.

Stefan wondered about Katya, beautiful Katya with her flaming red hair. Was she still living with his aunt or was she married and gone? He remembered how upset his mother had been when Sofie had adopted the girl.

Then there was his father…Stefan knew he had disappointed his father. He wasn't the student he should have been at school in Zagreb, nor was he as interested in the day to day running of the lands, which his father thought so necessary. Also, there had been some bad feelings before Stefan left because he found out that Ivan Balaban was his father's son and not just his father's godson. The memory was still a bit painful for he remembered his harsh words to his father. But…that was two years ago! He was confident that he would repair any damages made to the relationships with his mother and father. They would forgive him just as they always had in the past. Now he would be a loving son, a model son. He would be whatever they wanted him to be. He brought with him earrings more beautiful and valuable than the ones he stole from his mother to pay his gambling debt. In his mind he had often pictured how pleased his mother would be when she saw the replacement earrings he had for her.

The memory of the Turk made Stefan feel uneasy. Those cold dark eyes, set in that round unsmiling face, had greatly frightened him. Stefan had been so frightened of the Turk, that he in a panic had taken his mother's heirloom earrings as payment. Then, because the payment had been one day late, the Turk had demanded more money. It was at this same time that the gossip and scandal spread through the village when his father admitted to being Ivan Balaban's father. It had been too much. Too much for an insecure young man to handle, so he escaped through the forest away from the furor, and away from his mother who seemed on the verge of madness.

Now, he was no longer an insecure young man dependent on his father for money. Stefan had money and he had lots of it!

He pulled a gold Swiss watch from his pocket, its cover beautifully enameled in soft colors. The musical sounds of a waltz escaped when the cover was opened to show the time. The face of the watch was mother of pearl with hand painted numerals. He smiled as he looked at the valuable watch. To Stefan's delight, the former owner of the watch used it to cover a bet and proved to be a poor card player.

CHAPTER 2

In the large two-story house, Anton Vladeslav, Stefan's father, hesitated before descending the stairs leading to the dining room. Still a handsome man, with a touch of grey at his temples, he looked back towards his sister Sofie's room, the room she had before she married and left for Trieste. Sofie and her husband, Alexie, were stopping at her childhood home on their way to Zagreb, where they hoped to find a doctor who would tell them why Sofie was so ill. She had no faith in the doctors of Trieste. None of the Italian doctors could cure her first love, Vincent, those many years ago. Remembering how Vincent was not saved, Sofie insisted that Alexie bring her back to Croatia, where she trusted the doctors.

Katya, whom she loved as a daughter and had legally adopted, put aside her very harsh feelings of the people of Vladezemla and made the journey from Trieste only to please Sofie. It was Katya's knowledge of herbal healing which made the superstitious peasants wary of her, not only labeling her a witch, but blaming Katya for all the unhappiness in their quiet village.

Once it was known that the Turk was the man she had escaped from, the man her brother-in-law had sold her to, Katya was blamed for the Turk's attack on Stefan's mother. Some even speculated that the Turk had also attacked Ivan Balaban. But most of the gossip staunchly maintained that it was his half-brother Stefan who did it. Whenever the villagers talked about such things, and they did often, they would mention that these unwelcome events came about only after Katya had arrived. In their minds before her arrival, all had been peaceful and happiness had comforted them all like a warm blanket.

Anton's concern for his sister Sofie's health was deeply etched on his troubled face. He slowly descended the stairs, where at the foot of the steps waited Klara, the housekeeper. She was frustrated that her old knees kept her from climbing to the second floor to visit Sofie.

"How is she?" Klara was dressed in her usual white homespun full skirt and long sleeved blouse. A light brown braid was coiled atop her head like a crown. Being an unmarried woman, she didn't have her hair covered.

"Did she ask for coffee? I can get some coffee." Klara wanted to do something…anything to help. The woman's soft brown eyes were moist with tears of worry for her childhood friend. She silently cursed her aching knees.

"I don't think she wants any coffee." said Anton with a heavy sigh, leaning against the wall.

"Oh, Klara, she looks awful." His voice was filled with dread.

The sudden opening of the door surprised them both. It was as if a great wind had blown it open. The startled pair stared as an excited and smiling Stefan ran towards them. He dropped his carpet bag running past the dining table to his father. "Tata, I am home!" He cried, throwing his arms around his father giving the shocked man a bear hug. "I am so glad to be home." Stefan whispered as he held onto his speechless father.

"Sveta Maria," cried Klara, "Holy Mary, it can't be you!"

In his excitement, Stefan didn't notice that his father did not return his own enthusiastic hug. He let go of his father and wrapped his arms around the wide eyed Klara.

"Hug me, Klara," he said. And hug him, she did. She had not liked him as a spoiled child or when he was a young student in Zagreb, but now the old housekeeper hoped his appearance meant the return of some happiness and normalcy to Vladezemla.

No bright smile shone on the father's face as he looked with disappointment at Stefan and the teary-eyed Klara.

Anton's voice reflected no happiness as he said, "You are alive." He studied Stefan, looking him up and down. "And you seem to be doing well by the clothes you wear." Now his tone was cool, "For two years we worried, prayed and cried thinking you were dead. Not one letter to let us know that you were alive."

A bewildered Stefan stared at his father. This was not the reception Stefan had expected. He noticed that his father looked older and that he was wearing the peasant white pantaloons and long over shirt, instead of the fine riding clothes Stefan remembered. In his mind he had anticipated happiness, back slapping, kissing, tears of joy, drinks being passed around to celebrate his homecoming, but, not this…this indifference.

Hurt by this reception, Stefan cleared his throat nervously. He looked about the room. It was as he had remembered it. There was the large rectangular dining table with the high-backed chairs in place. Strange that it wasn't set for breakfast. Where was his Mamitza? She would be happy to see him! He smiled at the thought of her, for he had been her whole life. Nothing he had ever done had lessened her love for him.

"Where is Mamitza?" he asked, looking around for his mother.

A worried Klara said nothing, only looked from Anton to Stefan.

After a long pause, giving Klara a warning look not to speak, Anton said, "She is in the chapel garden."

Without a word, Stefan ran passed Klara through the kitchen, startling the cook pounding bread dough on the table.

The kitchen door slammed behind Stefan as he jumped over the steps and hurried to the chapel beyond the kitchen garden.

"Oh, Anton…how could you?" asked a heartsick Klara,

"Mind your own business," snapped Anton.

"This family is my business." said Klara, wiping away tears with her sleeve. "I am not only a servant. I grew up in that kitchen, along with you and Sofie. I was here when you married Ernesta and I wiped that boy's bottom when he was a baby."

Anton's voice sounded tired, "Be quiet, old woman." He turned his back to her and slowly ascended the stairs, back to his sister's room.

CHAPTER 3

With a coffee cup in hand, a heavy hearted Klara seated herself at the table. So many arguments had taken place around this table in the past. Stefan's mother, Ernesta, unhappy in her marriage, fought Anton constantly over his generosity to Marko Balaban and Marko's family. Marko was Klara's cousin and had been as close as a brother to Anton. Sofie and Anton's mother had died when they were very young, so Klara's mother, then the cook at Vladezemla, cared for the Vladeslav children along with her own Klara and nephew Marko. Sofie and Anton, and the children of the household help, grew up together loving one another as if they were related. Though the four of them were close and had a strong bond, Klara and Marko knew their place. Marko never took advantage of their friendship. Klara, on the other hand, overstepped herself often making her feelings known when, as a servant, she should have remained quiet. She had worked in the kitchen from the time she was a girl of twelve. Her mother died leaving the capable Klara to become the household cook.

Ernesta had resented how comfortable Klara was with Anton and his sister, Sofie. Klara sometimes sat down at the table with them when Ernesta was not close by. Whenever Ernesta approached the dining room, Klara bustled back into the kitchen, leaving Anton and Sofie with guilty smiles on their faces.

There were times when Klara wondered where she would go if she were turned out by Ernesta. The old housekeeper was especially concerned about her position just before the truth that Ivan Balaban was Anton's biological son had become common knowledge. She had planned to ask her cousin Marko and his wife, Vera, if she could stay with them, but when Stefan left and the Turk appeared, she never thought anymore about leaving.

Now the sounds of heavy footsteps bouncing off the stairs grabbed Klara's attention. Sofie's wonderful husband, Alexie, was practically leaping over the steps as he descended.

"He's in the chapel garden," called out Klara, as the figure of Alexie flew past her. She heard the kitchen door slam with a bang.

Klara noticed her hand tremble slightly as she brought the cup to her lips. Alexie would make things right. Alexie Lukas had stolen all their hearts when he married Sofie. Alexie's father had been the family advokat, lawyer. When the older Lukas passed away, Alexie took over any legal matters for the Vladeslav family. It was when he came to draw up the legal papers allowing Sofie to adopt Katya that Sofie started to fall in love with the steady, strong Alexie. He was always polite, never intrusive, had a brilliant legal mind and even under the most stressful events remained calm and in control.

Klara was sure Alexie would know how to handle this new situation.

Nearing the chapel, Alexie heard Stefan before he saw him. The young man was on his knees sobbing. A stone cross marked his mother's grave with purple violets blanketing the ground.

A nervous Alexie stood quietly waiting for Stefan to compose himself. Flowering peach and apple trees pleasantly scented the warm air. On the gentle breeze came the familiar scents from the field below where the Gypsies camped. There was the smell of camp fires and meat roasting over open flames. Even the faint whinny of a horse was carried by the breeze.

Stefan sensed he was not alone. Embarrassed and angry by the intrusion, Stefan turned to the figure standing near.

"What are you doing here?" he demanded. Words caught in his throat as he continued, "This… is a very private moment…please leave."

"Please don't be embarrassed." Alexie's voice was soothing.

"I am here to tell you what happened." Alexie remained standing as he spoke. "I am Alexie Lukas, your aunt Sofie's husband." He extended his hand, which Stefan ignored.

Stefan rose from his knees. *His aunt's husband…his old maid aunt had a husband?*

23

CHAPTER 4

In a comforting tone, Alexie said, "Come let's sit. We will talk. So much has happened since you left."

Again Stefan ignored Alexie's extended hand. Stefan hesitated, confused, not sure what to do next. He stared out over the hills. Finally he sat beside Alexie on the wooden bench.

Alexie always looked neat. Even with his shirt tail out and his collar unbuttoned, he looked well put together. His dark brown hair was combed straight back, his mustache always neat and his brown eyes were full of warmth and compassion.

Looking closely at Alexie, Stefan recognized the lawyer. "I remember you. You are the family lawyer. The advokat who helped Sofie adopt Katya."

"Yes, I am. And," Alexie added, "I am Sofie's husband and we now live in Trieste."

Trieste? Stefan didn't understand. Why was Sofie in Trieste? Stefan remembered that Sofie often visited there. But, that could wait. He wanted to know about his mother.

Stefan took a cigarette case from his pocket. His hand trembled as he offered the open case to Alexie. Seeing Stefan's unsteady hands, Alexie took two cigarettes. Stefan watched as the older man lit them both with a tiny Italian match, then handed one to Stefan.

"Thank you," said Stefan, embarrassed that Alexie saw his trembling hands. For awhile the two men sat silently smoking.

Far away sounds of music and the sound of cow bells broke the silence in the quiet graveyard. Somewhere a dog barked. Birds twittered back and forth. A sparrow lighted on Ernesta's headstone, turning its head, as if it too was waiting to hear Alexie speak.

Alexie waited for Stefan to relax.

Minutes passed. Stefan did not look at Alexie, but stared far out into the forest beyond the chapel garden. It was on the forest road, high on the hill, he had traveled the day he escaped from Vladezemla. Should he have stayed? Could he have stayed with his mother so close to madness…when she was talking about murder? It was when

Sofie adopted Katya that Ernesta feared Stefan would not get his share of the land.

"*We could kill them you know.*" His mother had said. The look in her eyes and the sound of her voice had frightened him. The memory of that moment made him feel sick.

Stubbing out his cigarette on the sole of his boot, Stefan took a deep breath. "Tell me," he said, "tell me what happened to my mother."

CHAPTER 5

Picking up a slender twig from the ground, Alexie made designs in the dirt avoiding Stefan's eyes.

"We, the family, have talked about that night often," he began.

"The night she died?" asked Stefan.

"No…the night it started." Alexie cleared his throat. It was obvious he was nervous. How do you tell a young man that it was his gambling debt that brought about the misfortune of that terrible night? How could Alexie find the words that would not give this young man more pain than he already felt upon finding his mother's grave?

"Let me see," started Alexie. "The first time we saw the Turk was when we were coming home from Father Lahdra's."

Stefan's head jerked up in surprise. His voice was almost shrill, "The Turk was here? He came to the house?"

"As I understand it," explained Alexie, "the Turk was demanding more money which your mother refused to give him."

Stefan shook his head in disbelief. He hadn't thought the Turk would come to his home to confront his parents.

Alexie continued, "He was leaving the grounds as we were approaching. The Turk did not recognize Katya, but she recognized him. She became so upset that we could barely calm her."

This confused Stefan. "Why was she upset?" he asked.

"Because," said Alexie, "he was the man who bought her when she was in her village of Selna." .

Wide eyed, Stefan said, "It was the Turk she was hiding from?"

"Yes, and it appears he returned later that same night to rob the house. He must have thought everyone was down at the Gypsy camp for the festivities. But your mother and Katya stayed home. Katya was so upset at seeing the Turk that she refused to visit the Gypsies with us." He paused, sighed and went on. "Perhaps things would have worked out differently had they been with us."

Nervously, Stefan reached again in his pocket for his cigarette case. Alexie watched as Stefan lighted the cigarette before continuing his story.

"We don't know exactly what happened. We do know that the Turk had Katya and was leaving with her in a wagon. He had her face and head completely covered. Your father, who also stayed behind, was in the chapel. Upon hearing the wagon, he went to the road. He saw the Turk and tried to stop him, but the Turk was determined to run him over."

Stefan's face turned pale. *What danger had he brought to his family?* His voice caught as he asked, "Did he hurt my father?"

"It was a miracle." said Alexie. "One of Valina's Gypsies thought he heard something unusual and came up to the house. He saw the Turk try to run your father over with the horses. He jumped on the wagon and stabbed the Turk in the back."

This was the story everyone believed, but only the Gypsy, Mustafa, as he was called, knew the real story. He had actually been the Turk's accomplice. He stabbed the Turk when he saw the bracelet on Katya's wrist…the bracelet with its secret ancient symbols…the bracelet Queen Valina gave Katya as an amulet to keep her from harm. The shrewd Gypsy Mustafa knew Valina would be grateful and would reward him for saving Katya, so killing the Turk was to his advantage.

Stefan's hand shook as he took another draw on his cigarette. His voice sounded strained as he asked, "And my mother, where was she?"

Alexie rose, turned away, looked out over the hillside, avoiding Stefan's eyes. He wished he were upstairs with his wife, not down here telling this painful story to Stefan, who was visibly suffering.

Alexie turned to face Stefan, his own face expressing his reluctance to go on with the explanation of that terribly night's events. He wasn't sure how to go on. How does one comfort another man? With a woman one could take her hand, put a comforting arm around her shoulders…even hug her.

Alexie sat down next to Stefan and looked at him with eyes he hoped conveyed compassion.

He slowly began, "From the Gypsy camp we saw the wagon with horses galloping furiously towards the village driven by a Gypsy. In the wagon was the dead Turk, your injured father and a bleeding Katya." Here, Alexie, hesitated, clearing his throat, not sure how to go on.

"And my mother…where was my mother?"

"Oh, Stefan…" Alexie hesitated, now more than ever Alexie wished he were upstairs with Sofie, away from this unpleasant task. It was Anton who should be here telling his son the awful things that happened. It should be the father's place to explain this painful tale, to comfort his son, not an uncle…especially one who was not a blood relative.

"We don't know what happened to your mother. She may have had a stroke."

Alexie hurried on with the story. He wanted to get it over. He needed to be with Sofie…wanted to be with Sofie. He went on, "All the people who were at the Gypsy encampment were horrified thinking there may be bandits terrorizing the countryside. Once they heard there had been a murder, the people dispersed hurrying home for safety.

Sadly Alexie remembered that dreadful night when some of the men went back to Vladezemla.

"Several of us went up to the house. We found your mother on the floor. She was alive, but her arms and legs didn't work." Here he hesitated, searching for words that would not be too painful.

"We had to tie Ernesta to a chair which we put in the back of the wagon in order to bring her down to Marko Balaban's house."

Sofie and I, along with Father Lahdra and Klara followed the wagon on foot to Marko's house."

"But, I thought…"

Alexie interrupted Stefan. "Yes, you wonder how after Vera had confronted your father for revealing their youthful affair, we could be welcome in the Balaban home."

He told a pale faced Stefan how later, the Gypsies had found Ivan, bruised and battered, seemingly near death on the hillside and brought him home. How they all sat through the night watching Katya use her herbal skills to soothe Ivan's torn and tattered body. How Stefan's mother, still as a statue, was put in Vera and Marko's bed.

28

Stefan felt ill. He wanted to hear more, to hear about his mother, but knew he couldn't stand anymore, not now. His gambling debt had set off a series of terrible, unexpected events and he was sick with guilt. Stefan weakly raised a hand to waive off Alexie, to stop him from speaking.

Seeing how tortured Stefan was, how disturbed the young man had become, Alexie asked, "Would you rather we stopped for now? We can talk later when you feel better." With his face turned away from Alexie, Stefan gave a weak nod.

Alexie put a comforting hand on Stefan's shoulder. "I must get back to Sofie." He rose, reluctant to leave the distraught young man, yet eager to be at Sofie's side.

"We will talk more, when you are ready." he said. Then he was gone through the kitchen garden and up the three wooden stairs into the house and back to his beloved Sofie.

CHAPTER 6

"Tzervene kose tsoprenitza," Katya had heard this chant during her arrival to the Vladeslav house. Riding in the carriage with Alexie and Sophie, she had kept her eyes straight ahead, not wanting to see the faces saying the taunting words, "Red-haired witch." She heard it many times over. Oh, how she wanted to be back in Trieste, back with the woman she called Nona. Back where she loved being so close to the sea, hearing the comforting sound of the lapping water and the beauty of the curling waves as they found their way to the shore; feeling the sea breezes as they blew through the city, leaving the air smelling clean.

She was born Croatian, raised Croatian, but she felt at home in Trieste with its beautiful stone buildings overlooking the Adriatic. She loved the outdoor markets with their display of fresh flowers and the many baskets of fresh fish. She did not, however, like seeing the tiny dead birds, a delicacy sold by old women. The eels always fascinated her and to her surprise, she discovered that on more than one occasion, she had been served fried eel for dinner.

The church where Katya, Nona, Sofie and Alexie heard Mass in Trieste was Sant'Antonio Nuovo. Katya had no way of knowing that it had been a project of the Austrian Empress Maria Theresa or that it was completed in 1849. She only knew that she marveled at the beauty of the painted icons done by Venetian and German artists. High above, the church attic was decorated with the statues of local martyrs.

Today, she was seated in the small Vladeslav chapel with its simple wooden benches. There was a modest altar standing beneath a large crucifix with a sad-faced Christ who always seemed to be looking down upon Katya. This was a place of comfort for her. Here she had prayed and felt safe when she first arrived to Vladezemla two years ago. Now she was tucked back in a secluded corner with a book. She sat near a small window reading. In the chapel there was no one to call her tzoprenitza, witch. She only hoped that tomorrow, when Sofie went to the doctor, he would know what was wrong and their stay away from Trieste would be short. Katya was determined to stay in the Vladeslav house or this chapel until it was time to go home and home for her meant Trieste.

She heard the chapel door open then close, briefly throwing light into the center of the room. Katya watched as a figure walked slowly to the altar. In the dim light, she couldn't make out who it was. She heard a man moan, "Boze Moy…My God". The voice repeated it again.

On the stone altar stood a lovely etched red glass chimney protecting the tall burning candle within. Beside it were several small candles and a rectangular metal tray two inches deep, filled with soft soil. The man picked up a candle and lighted it from the larger burning candle. She saw his face illuminated by the candle…it was Stefan! He looked different. His curly hair was smooth and he now had a mustache, but she knew it was Stefan! Everyone thought he was dead, but here he was! She watched him pick up another candle and light it. He stood it up in the earth filled pan alongside the first candle.

What should she do? She wanted to leave, but when he cried out again, "Boze Moy…My God," this time in a tortured voice, she froze in place.

"God forgive me…what has happened because of me?" He fell onto the nearest bench, burying his face in his hands. "Mamitza forgive me." He pleaded aloud. "Forgive me for going away…and…forgive me for loving Magda the way I should have loved you."

Katya was embarrassed to hear Stefan's anguish. She didn't want to be there. She wished she could melt into the bench. She prayed he wouldn't see her. She barely breathed.

Now Stefan was speaking to the Christ figure on the crucifix. "I came home to be a good son. I needed to make my Mamitza happy again and to show Tata that I could be the son he wanted."

He stood up agitated still speaking to the crucifix, "Somehow I can make things work with Ivan. He must feel as confused and hurt as I do." Stefan said, "We'll work it out."

Then softly, he said, "I miss Magda. I never had such a friend. She taught me so much." He spread his hands on the altar and leaned on it for support. After a moment he pushed himself away, he made the sign of the cross, turned quickly leaving the chapel. He never saw the wide eyed Katya hidden in the back corner of the chapel.

After a few seconds, Katya took a deep breath, for she barely breathed while watching Stefan. With some surprise she realized she felt deeply sorry for him. She once believed she could never forgive him for that time he came drunk into her room when she first had come to Vladezemla. That was two years ago. She had liked him back then, even thought he might have liked her. But when he came that night, he was drunk and he took her. Took her, not with love, but with lust!

Now, here she was staring at the two candles he had lit for his mother and someone else. She was feeling sorry for him, wanting to comfort him. *What was happening to her?*

CHAPTER 7

When Stefan came through the kitchen, into the dining room, Klara rose from her chair and hugged him.

"Come, sit with me," she said, as she settled back in her chair.

An ashen-faced Stefan sat across the table from the teary-eyed Klara. A bottle of slivovica and glasses stood in the center of the table.

Klara pushed a small glass to Stefan and took one herself.

"You pour." she said.

They each took a sip of the plum brandy.

"Klara...did I do all this?" He became emotional and couldn't continue. He shook his head and looked down.

Klara reached across the table, patting his hand. "Stefan...Stefan," she repeated. "Don't blame yourself. This was Destiny at work...or maybe God."

She continued, "Perhaps Destiny or God sees to it that we get the life we deserve." When she saw the pained look on his face, she went on, "You see, you aren't the only one who feels guilt over your mother's death. Your father feels a lot of guilt, though he doesn't admit it. He tries to find others to blame for what happened."

"But, why should he feel guilty?" asked Stefan, picking up his brandy glass, taking a sip.

"Because he never loved your mother the way he should have. He never let go his youthful romance with Vera Balaban and in his mind made that into something bigger than it was. And of course there was Ivan, the constant reminder that their romance had produced a son." she said, taking another sip of the slivovica.

"Tell me Klara, how did my mother die?" Stefan felt comfortable with Klara, more so than he had with Alexie. "I need to know."

"We don't know what happened to her that terrible night, the night the Turk came." She pointed to the stairs. "Your father found her on the floor...there." She pointed to the foot of the stairs. "She was like a rag doll. Nothing on her body worked. If you lifted her arm, it would fall." She demonstrated lifting her own arm then letting it drop. "We had several doctors come from Zagreb, but none could help." She pointed to the parlor, "We turned that into her room. During the day we had your mother tied to the chair so that she wouldn't fall off. We had a bed made up nearby as it was too difficult to get her upstairs. Your Ta's study was made into a room for the nurses who came and went."

"Nurses?" Stefan's eyes widened.

"Yes, your father thought he could take care of your mother himself, but it was too hard. He barely slept caring for her." Here she paused and smiled at Stefan. "You would have been proud to see how devoted he was to Ernesta. He insisted on feeding her, but she had trouble swallowing. He was becoming thin with worry and frustration. This went on for fourteen months. Then one morning when it was time to get her up and dressed...she didn't wake. She was gone."

Klara poured more slivovica in Stefan's glass and topped off her own.

"It was a blessing when she died. Even when she was alive she wasn't really with us."

Stefan felt very calm. Perhaps it was the way Klara spoke to him, or it could be the slivovica, or perhaps hearing that his father had been so wonderful in caring for Mamitza. Whatever it was, Stefan, felt better...more relaxed.

"Anton was starting to be more himself, pleasant again." continued Klara. "The loss of you and Ernesta seemed to fade just a little. But," she sighed deeply, "when Father Lahdra died a month ago and Sofie got so ill, Anton's mood darkened."

"How did he...Lahdra die?" asked Stefan.

"We aren't sure. Maybe his horse threw him or he fell. The Sokach brothers found him dead on the road one morning on their way to the fields."

"Lahdra was Ta's dearest friend." said Stefan softly. "It is as though he has lost everybody." He paused, "What about Marko Balaban? Are they still friends...after...after..."

"Oh, the gossip was terrible!" declared Klara. "But, now and then, Marko comes here and we play cards, talk about the old times when we were children together." She wiped a stray tear from her eye, "Oh, but we miss Sofie. We don't see her often enough now that she lives in Trieste."

"Why did they move to Trieste?" asked Stefan, "Doesn't Alexie have his advokat office in Zagreb?"

"Not anymore. He closed it. Now he and Sofie own the Renaldi Trading Company."

This news came as a surprise to Stefan. "I came through Trieste on the way here." said Stefan. "I would have liked seeing it." Then he asked, "Who is in charge, now that they are here?"

"Alexie's assistant Ruda Klarich packed up and went to Trieste to work with them."

"This makes no sense." said Stefan. "What made them want to leave?"

"The company belonged to the mother of the man Sofie wanted to marry when she was a young girl. Your grandfather, who you never knew, sent your father to bring her home. Vincent Renaldi was ill and died before your father got there."

Interrupting their conversation, a thin young woman came from the kitchen. She was wearing a full homespun skirt and long sleeved blouse gathered at the neck. In her hand she carried a platter of fresh warm bread sprinkled with sugar. Her face was plain and long. Over her brown braids she wore the mandatory scarf of a married woman.

"Hvala, Zora. Thank you." Waving her hand towards Stefan, she said, "This is Gospodine's son, Stefan. He has come home."

The shy woman only nodded, quickly placed the fragrant bread on the table and retreated to the kitchen.

Back to the subject, Stefan said, "I still don't understand why they moved to Trieste."

"Because," explained Klara, "Lucia Kurecka gave them the company." Seeing the bewildered look on Stefan's face, she continued. "The old woman always loved Sofie and even after her son Vincent died, she wanted Sofie to come and live with her. I don't know what happened the last time they visited Trieste, but something made Alexie and Sofie decide to stay and get married there. All of this distressed your father still more."

"I should go see Teta Sofie," said Stefan, rising. "I probably should have gone before this, but I was so upset needing to know what had happened."

"Go see her. I can't get up the stairs or I would be with her. Kiss her for me."

CHAPTER 8

Leaving the chapel, a confused Katya walked to the wooden bench which encircled the large tree across from the main entrance of the house. It was under this tree that Stefan helped her with her reading lessons when she first arrived from Selna.

She sat on the bench and leaned against the trunk of the tree, smoothing her ankle length green skirt. The long-sleeved blouse, gathered and tied at the throat matched the skirt. The clothes she had from Trieste were more in the continental fashion and very different from the embroidered homespun clothes worn in the villages of Croatia.

As she sat there looking at the house, Katya's thoughts kept returning to Stefan and what she had witnessed in the chapel. Watching him pray, for that's surely what it had been…touched something deep inside of her. She had never witnessed another's such intimate moment.

Across from the tree was the front entrance of the house where Klara appeared at the doorway. She waved as she made her way across the yard, limping slightly because of her sore knees.

The old woman sat beside Katya and said, "Stefan is home." When she didn't get a surprised reaction, Klara looked hard at the silent girl. "So, you are not surprised that he is home? Home, when we all thought he was dead?"

In a low voice, Katya said, "I saw him in the chapel. Oh, Klara, I almost cried…he seemed so sad."

"What did he say to you?"

"He didn't see me," said Katya. "I was in the back of the chapel. I would have left, but I couldn't intrude on his prayers…that is, I think he was praying."

"He doesn't seem the spoiled boy anymore, does he?" Klara shooed at a persistent fly buzzing about her round face.

Klara said, "We spoke about his mother and how she was ill. I also told him about his father and how devoted he was to Ernesta."

"Where is Stefan now?" asked Katya.

"Upstairs, with Sofie," said Klara.

Thinking of Sofie, Katya said, "I feel as if I have failed Teta Sofie. I steeped herbs, I made potions. Nothing I did helped her feel better." Katya placed the book she was holding on the bench beside her. "I should be up there with them." she said, meaning Sofie and Alexie, "But I feel as if I am in the way. Alexie seems to suffer so holding her hand, wanting to do something to make her feel better."

"Are you going to Zagreb with them to see the lechnik, the doctor?"

"I would like to," said Katya.

Klara rose from the bench with some effort. "These old knees of mine!" she said. "I had better see how many we will have for supper. Possibly Alexie will want to eat with Sofie. I'll see you at supper." And she was gone, taking slow painful steps across the yard to the house.

Far back away from the house were the fields, livestock and a large barn. This is where the men who worked for Anton could be found. Not all of them used the common road to go home, for some it was quicker to cut across their neighbor's fields.

In the distance, Katya could see a figure heading towards her on his way to use the main road into the village. She watched as the man walked slowly using a cane. It was only when he came very close that Katya surprised, realized it was Ivan.

She stood up waiting for him to reach her. When he came very near, she could see his shy smile. He looked older and more tired than when she last saw him. His light brown hair was a bit longer than she remembered, but his brown, gold-flecked eyes were the same and he was still handsome.

"May I sit down?" he asked, smiling.

"Of course," she said, pleased to see him. She watched as he balanced on his strong leg and dropped onto the bench. His kept the weak leg extended.

Katya felt her eyes grow moist. Once, she thought she loved him. That seemed so long ago. Still she felt a flutter in her stomach. She remembered how she and his sister-in-law, Luba tended him throughout that night when the Gypsies found him on the hillside all bruised and torn. That night, thinking he might die, she thought that she loved him, wanted him.

When Ivan was better, he and Katya were sure they were meant for one another. It was then that his mother, Vera, had sent Katya away.

"We don't want a witch in the house." She had lied, telling Katya that Ivan believed she had used witchcraft to make him fall in love with her. "He wants you to leave." And a confused, broken hearted Katya did leave.

Now, two years later, Ivan stared at his beloved Katya. At last she had returned. She had left without a word to him.

Her wild red hair, that he had loved so much, was now neatly coiled in a bun at the nape of her neck. Her skin was still flawless and her eyes were green emeralds, just as he had remembered them.

Katya was the first to speak. 'How are you?"

"I get along. I guess I am fine." He said, staring at her face, her eyes, and her slender throat.

Looking at his extended leg she asked, "When did this happen?"

"That night when the Gypsies found me," he said.

Is it possible she is more beautiful? Ivan tried not to stare into her eyes.

"How is it I didn't discover it?" She was apologizing and explaining at the same time. "I searched your entire body and didn't feel any broken bones." Then she said, "If I had stayed longer, maybe I would have discovered it."

Ivan took Katya's small hand in his work rough hand. "I know why you left. It took a long time to get my mother to admit she sent you away." Now he was looking deep into those green pools she had for eyes, "How was it you believed her? Believed that I could think you were a witch?"

Tears welled in her eyes. "Everyone thought I was a witch. They still do. It was too much for me...I am sorry that I didn't at least say good-by."

"I would have come to Trieste for you, if I had been able." He pointed to his bad leg, touching it with his cane. "Whatever was damaged didn't heal correctly, but at least I am able to walk."

"Are you going to walk all the way home down that steep road?" She asked concerned.

"I do it every morning and evening. I can't let myself become weak." he explained.

"Do you still ride a horse?" she asked.

"Sometimes, but the movement bothers me here." He pointed high on his thigh.

As a healer, Katya wanted to touch his leg, to see where the problem was but she felt she shouldn't.

The wind started picking up, swirling small puffs of dust about. The mean sky darkened as putty colored clouds gathered in an angry mass.

"I should be going," said Ivan. "It looks as if it might rain."

So lost were they in their conversation, they didn't notice Stefan standing a few yards away from them. It was as though they were discovering each other all over again, oblivious to what was around them. Only the gathering wind caught their attention.

Stefan frowned at the sight of Ivan's protruding leg and the cane, his gaze went to Katya. Were they lovers? Were they married? Since his return, no one had told him about Katya or Ivan.

"Hello you two," he said, taking Katya's hand and touching it to his lips. He smiled at his half brother remembering how he was jealous of him when Ivan was then, only the Godson. He shook Ivan's extended hand.

"You're back." Ivan said genuinely surprised and even a bit pleased. "We thought we would never see you again. We…that is, some of us thought something bad happened to you."

"No," said Stefan with an embarrassed smile. "I was just traveling."

The wind was stronger now, sending sharp bits of hardened dirt around them, stinging them. Leaves were dropping from the tree.

"Katya fought to hold her billowing skirts down, "Ivan, you can't walk home in this wind. It will rain soon."

"Of course not," said Stefan. "Come we will go into the house. Klara is setting the table. We will have a wonderful dinner. It will be my coming home party."

Without waiting for a word from Ivan, Stefan helped his half-brother to his feet. Fighting the wind, he half carried the stumbling Ivan to the house. Katya with skirts swirling about her had Ivan's cane in one hand while shielding her eyes from the stinging wind with the other.

In the house, the old housekeeper's jaw dropped when she saw Ivan being helped into the room by Stefan. Bewildered, Klara remembering the bitter feelings Stefan had towards Ivan the day he left, couldn't believe Stefan was now almost carrying him into the house. Katya handed the cane to Ivan, and he steadied himself as Stefan let go of him.

"It's getting bad outside. Ivan can't walk home in this weather. He is staying for dinner with us," announced Stefan.

CHAPTER 9

A somber Anton, seated at the head of the table, surveyed the family. All of them smiling and chatting as if it were a normal occurrence. Alexie joined them for supper soon after Sofie had fallen asleep. Alexie sat opposite Anton, while Klara and Katya sat facing Stefan and Ivan.

Oil lamps placed on nearby tables lit the room, as did the candles in the center of the table. The tablecloth was white with crocheted edging, done long ago by Ernesta.

Klara was beaming with pleasure. This was the first time since that awful night when the Turk had invaded the house, that there was some laughter at the table. Only sadness and gloom had encompassed Klara and Anton for the last two years. Caring for the invalid Ernesta and worrying about the missing Stefan, had been a terrible strain on both of them. When Sofie moved to Trieste, it nearly broke Anton's heart for he had felt abandoned. Then it became worse seeing Ivan crippled from his fall.

Believing that Stefan had attacked Ivan causing Ivan's leg to be crippled gnawed at their father.

Now, here at dinner, it annoyed him to see all of them happy and laughing.

Zora, the cook, normally would not have been pleased to prepare enough food for such a crowd. Zora usually made a small meal that Klara could warm up and serve after Zora had gone home to her own family.

But, tonight was exciting! Here she was in the midst of Vladezemla's most prominent and talked about family. She was serving the mysterious Stefan sitting alongside the brother he was supposed to have attacked and across from him sat the 'witch.' Zora was careful not to look at Katya with more than a glance for fear that Katya would put a spell on her.

The rain outside pounded the house. The bright flash of lightening lit up the night as if it were daylight followed by wall rattling claps of thunder. The superstitious cook was sure that Katya had some evil reason for making the storm appear.

Instead of sitting in the kitchen until she was needed, Zora stood in the dining room. Standing next to the kitchen door, she could see and hear everything. Her skin tingled with excitement. Looking at Anton, she was especially aware of the dark mood that surrounded the master of the house.

Anton glowered at Stefan. After a while Anton said, his voice cold, "How can you laugh and be so gay, so soon after hearing of your mother's death?"

The room went silent. The only sound was that of thunder and the rain beating on the windows.

All eyes were on Anton.

"And," he went on, "how is it that your carpet bag is so full of money and jewels?"

For the first time since he was home, Stefan thought of his carpetbag. It was always by his side when he traveled, but here at home, he forgot about it.

Stefan rose from his chair. He looked around the table. He looked at each one in turn, deep into their eyes. Each looked back in silent wonder. His gaze stopped at his father.

"Alright, I will tell you where I have been." But first he drained his wine glass in one steady gulp.

"I have been traveling with Magda Petrovich." Seeing no sign of recognizing the name, he added, "Magda of Magda's gambling house in Zagreb." He said nothing of the girls available upstairs, but the look on his father's face and Alexie's made it clear they knew.

Before anyone interrupted, he went on. "We traveled throughout Italy and France and sometimes Spain. We supported ourselves by gambling."

CHAPTER 10

When Stefan finished telling them where he had been and what he had been doing, he expected all sorts of comments, instead it was only Ivan who spoke.

"Tell me," asked Ivan, less interested in Stefan's adventures with Magda, and more about the last time he saw Stefan on the hillside road. "When we saw each other on the day you left, did we speak? I can't remember."

Before replying, Stefan glanced around the table. He looked at his family and felt a sense of affection for them that he had never experienced before.

The boredom and contempt of his youth had been replaced by something new and wonderful. He was connected to all these people. They were all part of him.

The great loss of Magda...his mentor, his friend, his other mother, had left a huge emptiness in him. Instead of a loving reunion, he found his own mother dead and buried. It made the hole in his heart even larger. But, like a miracle, that hole was closing. Here was his family! He wasn't alone. Whatever hurt and jealousy Stefan may have felt as a youth, he had a brother...his half brother, Ivan.

The look on old Klara's face reflected the look he had hoped to see on his Mamitza's face, a look of love and happiness.

The old housekeeper's eyes glistened as she looked around the table. *They were a family again!* No longer was it just Klara and Anton, two old unhappy people sharing the house sitting down to lonely meals. Klara could feel the new energy in the room...young people were back. The house would be alive again.

Katya and Alexie with smiles on their faces appeared happy with Stefan's company. Everyone seemed pleased around the table, with the exception of his father. Displeasure hardened Anton's face.

Before Stefan could answer Ivan, Anton spoke. It was meant for everyone at the table. "Stefan has been in the bad company of a Madam for two years." He looked with disdain at Stefan. "He has been traveling and living with her, soiling the Vladeslav name."

Stefan started to speak, but Anton raised his hand to silence him. Rising from his chair, Anton looked fiercely at his son, "You tried to kill Ivan and now you dare sit at my table as if you are still part of this family!"

The room went dead silent. The harshness of the words broke the cheerful mood like water on fire. All eyes were fixed on Anton.

Zora the cook, still standing like a statue at the kitchen door, stared with eyes the size of saucers. *Boze Moy, My God*, she said to herself, over and over. It was all she could do to keep from running home and telling her family and everyone else in the village what she was witnessing. She was tingling with excitement.

Stephan sat down, next to his half brother with his eyes fixed on Ivan. "Ivan..." his voice was low, hushed. "Why do they all think I harmed you?" Stefan's face reflected a mixed look of confusion and pain. "I saw you seated on the hillside. I only paused long enough to look at you. When you said nothing, I walked on."

Ivan rose somewhat unsteady, his hands on the table for support. Stephan also stood up. The men, half brothers, looked intently at one another.

Katya and the others held their breath fearing what might come next.

Ivan spoke, his words slow and soft. "I remembered seeing you." He hesitated, "When everyone asked me what happened, all I could remember was that I saw you." Ivan dropped his eyes, "I never said that you hit me."

Stefan looked deep into Ivan's eyes, "I swear I did you no harm. I never touched you." Then to everyone's astonishment he added, "Bratso, Brother, I swear I never struck you!"

Stefan offered his hand to Ivan. Ivan ignored the extended hand. Instead he wrapped his arms around his half brother, who as a boy had greatly resented him. Now, at last they were brothers.

A happy chaos erupted at the table. Everyone, but Anton was in a group around the brothers. Bewildered, Anton dropped into his chair. *What had he done? How could he have believed his Stefan capable of attempted murder?*

45

A crying Klara wrapped her arms around the two men, who in her heart were still the boys she watched as they grew to manhood. Alexie's eyes were moist and he wished Sofie had been in the room to witness this moment. When Klara let go of the two brothers, Alexie warmly shook each of their hands and excused himself to go to Sofie's room, hoping to find her awake so he could tell her the news.

With a tear streaming down her cheek, Katya kissed Ivan on the cheek, and she kissed Stefan, brushing his cheek lightly with her fingers.

No one noticed sad Anton as he quietly rose from his chair and with a heavy heart, walked through the kitchen door, through the garden to the comfort of his chapel.

The storm had settled into a gentle rain, somewhat like the verbal storm that had been in the dining room and was now past.

Zora was not missed from her post outside the kitchen door. She was running through the slowing rain, jumping wildly over puddles and splashing through mud. She had NEWS...news that would excite the villagers, further undermining the Vladeslav's once-respected reputation.

CHAPTER 11

The slim blond priest rode his brown horse to Vladezemla. He was a stranger in these parts and lonely. He wore black trousers, a black shirt with a white collar and crucifix at his neck. Instead of a cassock, he wore a black jacket. On his head was a brimmed black hat.

Those he passed along the road respectfully nodded. He was their priest, but not yet their friend or loving pastor as Lahdra had been. Father Lahdra had been the pastor of Sveti Josif Cerkva, Saint Joseph's Church for sixteen years. He had baptized many of them, buried more of them and prayed with all of them. He had been part of the village.

Father Mika Orlich knew he was a stranger to the people here. He hoped he could win them over and be not only their priest, but their friend. Listening to the stories told by his housekeeper, Zlata, who had also been Lahdra's housekeeper, further depressed him. Plump Zlata, always with a babushka on her head, went on endlessly about how wonderful Father Lahdra had been; how kind, how he never made demands. She would go on and on, until Mika would leave the house and go to the church for some peace.

"Dear Father, help me be a good priest." He would pray. "Show me how to be the priest they want and need."

His pious praying did not go unnoticed by Zlata, who passed this information on to the villagers. No one remembered Father Lahdra spending so much time on his knees. Mika's praying made the villagers uncomfortable. Did the new priest expect such passionate devotion from them?

Mika was young, just out of the Archdiocesan Lyceum in Zagreb where he studied at the Theology Seminary.

He had heard how Anton Vladeslav had befriended Father Lahdra when Lahdra first came to Sveti Josef's, so Mika was disappointed that Gospodine Vladeslav had yet to invite him to his home.

However, today Mika had a very good reason to go to Vladezemla uninvited. While going through the desk at the parish

47

house, Mika came across a stack of ledgers tied with cord. Under the cord was a note which read: These are to go to Anton Vladeslav upon my death. The cord was sealed with wax in two places, anchoring the note. The wax seals were meant only to be broken by Anton.

Alexie, Sophie and Katya, were gone to Zagreb to see a doctor reputed to be excellent.

Alone, deep in thought, Anton stood in the chapel garden. While looking out at the field below where the Gypsies were camped, he could see the priest approaching. Terribly hurt by the loss of Lahdra, Anton was not ready to befriend the new priest, so he slipped unseen into the chapel.

The ledgers hanging from the saddle, bounced against Mika's knees. The horse gently navigated the cobbled road within the stone walls leading to the large weather-worn wooden house. Mika found the large house with two levels impressive. Once inside the stone wall, the first building Mika noticed was the small chapel made of stacked stones with its sturdy wooden door flanked by two small arched windows.

Mika's eyes were drawn to the large iron cross standing on the top of the chapel which was twisted and coiled, resembling the roots of a tree. In the center of the cross was a circle with iron tendrils radiating outward. The young priest had never seen a cross like this one, which had been made by Marko Balaban, Anton's childhood friend and the local blacksmith.

A huge shaggy dog blocked Mika's approach. Its loud barks frightened the priest and startled the horse, making it skittish.

"Stoy, stoy!" shouted Mika, trying to control his horse while it twisted away from the barking dog.

Stefan, hearing the commotion, ran from the house to the yard. He didn't recognize the large Tornjak, the mountain herding dog.

Stefan shouted, "Shuti, pas...quiet dog." To Stefan's surprise the large, furry white dog with its massive brown spotted head, stopped barking and dutifully went to Stefan's side, where he sat as if waiting for more instructions. Instinctively, Stefan reached down and patted the dog's head.

"I'm grateful you have such a well-trained dog." said the priest, aware his hands were trembling.

Stefan looked down at the now quiet beast, which looked up at him with large dark sparkling eyes, as if Stefan was his beloved master.

"Ah, well…" stammered Stefan. "Odi…go." He demanded waiving a hand at the dog. Dutifully the dog ambled up the step to the far side of the porch where he settled down for a snooze.

Stefan's attention returned to the stranger. "I am so sorry the dog startled you." Taking the reins from Mika's hands he said, "Let me help you."

Unseen, Anton watched from the chapel doorway, as Yura, a long time trusted worker came from the barn to lead Mika's horse away. Anton didn't want to meet Mika…he didn't want to meet anyone. He wanted to be left alone with his thoughts. He turned and went back into the chapel, the solitude wrapping him like a goose down comforter. He kept thinking about Stefan and how he shamefully had believed Stefan had harmed Ivan.

At the entrance of the house, Stefan said introducing himself "I am Stefan Vladeslav." He extended his hand to Mika.

"Father Mika Orlich." The men shook hands.

"Welcome to Vladezemla." Stefan took the bundle of books from the priest. Gesturing towards the door he said, "Come inside, please."

Mika looked warily at the dog who seemed content sleeping on the porch.

Klara was at the door as the men entered, her hair protected with a white babushka and a flour dusted apron was around her waist.

"Father Mika!" Klara was surprised to see him. "Is anything wrong? Has something happened?" She asked, wiping her hand on her apron before offering it in greeting.

"Nothing is wrong." He said taking her hand. "I just had something I needed to deliver."

Klara looked at the books in Stephan's hands.

"Here, let's not stand talking." Stefan nodded to the dining table. "Let's sit and talk." Nodding at Klara, he said, "Could we have some morning coffee and maybe some strudel? I can smell it. Is it ready to eat?"

Stefan placed the small stack of books on the table. He gestured for the priest to sit. Then sitting in a chair opposite Mika, he said, "Klara makes wonderful yabukah, apple strudel. She has been using up the stored apples from last fall.

Mika looked about the large dining room, which opened up to the living room area. He could see over the fireplace a lovely red Czechoslovakian etched vase and above that on the wall a fancy curved sword. The sturdy and comfortable furniture were a contrast to the basic wooden benches and chairs Mika had when at the seminary. He did have a nice velvet settee in the parish house, not knowing that it had been on loan from the Vladeslav's for Lahdra's use.

As Zora simultaneously poured the coffee and hot milk, in large cups, Mika looked at his host. He decided that Stefan was perhaps close to his own age, twenty, perhaps a little older. Stefan was wearing blue slim trousers, a white shirt open at the throat and a matching blue vest.

Father Mika removed his hat shoving it to the far end of the table.

Klara came bustling in with a huge platter of warm apple strudel sprinkled generously with sugar. Behind her was Zora with small plates, salvetes and forks. She placed a salvete...the napkin, beside each plate. After placing a generous serving of strudel on each plate, she returned to the kitchen.

Mika was a bit nervous, while Stefan appeared quite relaxed.

After a delicious mouthful of the apple treat, Mika said, "This is delicious. I didn't expect to taste any apples until the fall."

"We have a dug out space under the kitchen where we over-winter apples, cabbages, potatoes and other food." explained Stefan. "Not everything makes it through the winter."

Klara's return interrupted the conversation.

"May I join you?" Not waiting for a reply, she sat down with cup in hand.

Getting right to the point, she said, "There must have been a special reason for your visit."

Mika wasn't sure who Klara was. He knew she wasn't Stefan's mother, because he had heard the horrific story of the Turk's visit. Perhaps she was an aunt.

"I am here to see Gospodine Anton." Finishing his strudel he put down his fork, refusing more with a shake of his head, when Stefan offered it.

"You see," he went on, "I found these bound ledgers in a desk drawer."

Klara and Stefan looked at the slim volumes.

"There is a note affixed to the top." said Mika.

Stefan pulled the stack closer. Reading the note he said, "Lahdra wanted Tata to have these." Running his hand over the top book, he said, "I wonder why?"

Klara pulled off the babushka, lightly scratching her warm scalp.

"There must be something Lahdra wanted your Ta to know. They were the closest of friends." Looking at Mika she said, "Gospodine Anton misses Father Lahdra greatly." She dabbed her glistening eyes with a corner of the head scarf. "It was as if they were brothers. Now he feels he has no one."

Stefan caught the brief questioning look in Mika's eyes and explained, "I have been away for two years, but now I am here to stay." Stefan hoped this remark would prove to be true.

Not wanting to overstay his welcome as much as he enjoyed being in this house with Stefan and Klara, Mika said, "I must go now. I am sorry that I missed your father." he said, reaching for his hat as he rose from the chair. "Perhaps I will be welcome again."

"You are welcome, anytime." said Stefan. "On your next visit we can walk the grounds and I can show you Vladezemla."

Outside, Mika looked toward the chapel with its unusual twisted iron cross. "I believe I would like to see your chapel at another time."

Mika's horse watered and cooled down by Yura, now waited under the shade of the large tree across from the house.

The large dog rose from his place at the far end of the porch and stood beside Stefan, his head gently leaning against Stefan's leg. The dog no longer showed any aggressiveness. He appeared as a gentle family pet.

Mika mounted his horse and Stefan walked a few steps alongside the priest with the dog as his companion. With his last wave good-by Stefan sat on the wooden seat built around the tree. He pulled out his pack of Italian cigarettes. These cigarettes made in Florence were alright, but he preferred the nicely rolled and strong flavored Turkish ones.

As Stefan blew out a stream of smoke, he found himself scratching the head of the Tornjak, where it rested on Stefan's knee.

Where had it come from? Who did it belong to?

This sheep dog must belong to one of the workers, thought Stefan.

Stefan scratched the dog's v-shaped ears.

"What is your name, pas?" He asked the dog out loud.

The dog turned his head looking at Stefan, as if he understood.

Stamping out his cigarette on the sole of his boot, Stefan went to the house. The dog dutifully followed at his side. "Go on home." said, Stefan, waving the animal away. The dog sat before Stefan looking up at him affectionately.

With a laugh, Stefan walked through the door, leaving Pas, who quickly found a place on the porch to sleep and wait for Stefan's return.

CHAPTER 12

Zagreb, once a part of the Roman Empire, is a beautiful city displaying medieval buildings along with a white painted church with a tiled roof that stands out like a jewel.

The Crkva Sveti Marka, or St. Mark's Church was built in the 13th century, its colorful tiled roof depicting the Zagreb Coat of Arms and another for Croatia, Dalmatia and Slavonia.

The outdoor market is situated near St. Mark's church in the square, where villagers from various parts of the land sell or trade goods, food, and livestock.

Tamburitza music is heard in various parts of the area and the sound of it gives the square a festive air. Sometimes only one musician plays his prima or brach, elsewhere two or three men play together. Always, anywhere in Croatia, one might hear the music of the stringed instruments so loved by the Croatian people. The tambura was brought to Croatia centuries ago, possibly by the Turks. Tambura is a Turkish word.

The air is filled with the smells of food and one's eyes are dazzled by the array of clothing worn by the people mingling in the square. Each village or provence has a style or design of its own. Some costumes are heavily embroidered with geometric designs, while others are like a garden of flowers. Then, some are a simple, homespun white blouse and skirt trimmed in ribbons or lace. Leather shoes with turned up toes, hats with tassles, vests heavily embroidered in gold threads, and coins sewn on aprons can all be seen here. There are large fur hats on mustachioed men, swaggering with daggers at the hip. All are exciting to watch.

At an outdoor kafana, a tourist with a pad might be seen sketching a villager whose clothing especially catches the artist's eye.

Looking out at the city one could not imagine that it had been invaded by the Mongols, so much so, that between 1242 and 1261, defensive walls and towers were built to protect from anticipated Tatar raids.

53

Katya enjoyed none of the sights and sounds of the square. She was seated at a table under a shade tree, an untouched glass of tea before her. Her eyes were fixed on the door across the square which bore a sign: J. POPOVICH, Ljechnik.

To Kayta it seemed a very long time since Alexie and Sofie entered that door. So worried was Katya, that she didn't think about the last time she came through Zagreb; that time some two years ago, when Milan helped her escape from the Turk. She wasn't thinking about the excitement she had felt at the sights and sounds back then. She didn't remember the beautiful woman in the large yellow hat at the hotel entrance who had fascinated Katya with her gorgeous gown and the plume in her hat.

All she could do was worry about Sofie. What if Sofie were to die? Tears welled in Katya's eyes. Sofie was like a mother to her, perhaps the only person who loved Katya. She knew that Nona, in Trieste, loved her, but it was different with Sofie. Katya felt she and Sofie belonged together, belonged to one another.

Dear God, please let this doctor help Sofie. Let him cure her. Katya prayed silently, over and over. It had become her mantra. She even added, *I will never ask you for anything again.*

None of the potions or herbal teas Katya had administered to Sofie helped. With each passing day Sofie became more ill. She couldn't eat and when she did, most of the time she would throw up. Even some odors made her ill.

Seeing Dr. Popovich's door open, Katya, leapt from her chair, knocking over the glass of tea. She saw Alexie and Sofie emerging from the doctor's door. Katya could see Alexie's protective arm around Sofie's shoulders. Sofie held a handkerchief to her face and it was evident she was sobbing.

CHAPTER 13

"Why is this dog sleeping by the door? Who gave it water and food?" Anton pointed to the large dog, who looked up briefly, then dropped his head once more to the cool porch boards.

Klara said, "He showed up when the priest came." She shrugged her shoulders, "Maybe Yura knows who he belongs to. I'll send Zora to fetch him."

When Yura arrived from the barn he looked at the dog. Shaking his head, he said, "I don't know where he came from. First time I saw him was when he was barking at the priest." Yura walk around the dog, who raised his head looking at the three people staring at him. "Is it Stefan's dog?" asked Yura. "I saw Stefan petting him."

"Tie him up in the barn until we can find out who brought him here." said Anton. "Ask the men if anyone recognizes this dog."

An unhappy dog was dragged away from the house to the barn. He let his unhappiness be known, by howling as he was led away.

A greatly annoyed Anton found Stefan in the parlor looking over some books. "Do you hear that dog?" demanded Anton. "Where did he come from?"

Stefan was disappointed to see his once handsome father again dressed in the loose pantaloons and homespun shirt of the peasants. He so preferred seeing his father in the his tailored riding clothes.

Ignoring the question about the dog, Stefan said, "The priest, Father Mika, brought you these ledgers. Lahdra wanted you to have them."

Anton moved nearer to the table. He looked at the books a long time before resting a hand on the stack. "I can't read them." he said, his voice catching in his throat. He turned away quickly, before Stefan could see the tears in his eyes.

"Do something with that barking dog." Anton called over his shoulder as he left the room.

The moment Stefan entered the barn, the dog stopped barking, wagged his tail and if a dog could smile, it did.

Traveling in the cities of Italy and France, Stefan had almost forgotten the smells of the barn and its workers. The horses, the hay, and the garlic scented sweat of the men spread over him with a nostalgic wave. These smells had been part of his childhood as much as were the cooking smells wafting from the kitchen. How could he have hated it all when he was growing up? The rough, unshaven men were in the barn and on this land since he had been a small boy. It was as if they were his uncles.

Some came forward, removing their caps and extending a hand in greeting. Others, perhaps shy, only nodded.

Stefan smiled, shook their hands and found he was genuinely glad to be among these men who had been part of his childhood.

"Does anyone know who owns this dog?" he asked.

The men stood in a circle around the dog, murmuring and shaking their heads. No one recognized the dog.

"That is a fine dog." said a tall, thin man, with stubble on his face. "I could use a sheep dog."

"Good." said Stefan, "He is yours."

As the man approached the dog, they all heard a low menacing growl. All the men stepped back in fear. The man picked up a whip and hit the dog, showing it who was master. The dog let out with a high pitched yelp.

"Stop that!" Stefan grabbed the whip from the man's hand, flinging it to the ground. "Is that how you treat your animals?"

Without another word or look at the workers, Stefan untied the rope from the dog's neck. "Aide, Pas, come, dog." he said and turned away from the surprised men. The large Tornjak dog, obediently trotted behind Stefan towards the house.

Across from the entrance of the house, Stefan sat at the bench encircling the large tree trunk. He looked into the face of the dog. It was a beautiful Tornjak, a Croatian sheep dog. His strong square body covered in double fur ended with a tail held high, like a flag. The dog was white with reddish brown Irish spotting.

"What am I going to do with you?" Stefan asked the dog, who was now resting his huge head on Stefan's knee and looking up at Stefan. Stefan scratched the dog's head.

He had never had a dog of his own. There were dogs on Vladezemla, but none were considered pets. This dog, this pas, had chosen Stefan as his master.

"What am I going to do with you?" Stefan repeated. "I suppose you need a name." The dog pressed closer, his head still resting on Stefan's knee.

"You are a pas without a home, so I supposed I will call you, Pas." Pas lifted his head, looked up at Stefan. "If your owner comes to claim you, I will have to give you to him." It was as if the dog understood him. Pas laid on the ground next to Stefan and rested his head on Stefan's boot.

From the back of the property, Ivan came walking slowly towards the house, always limping slightly.

Stefan didn't notice Ivan because he was looking at the outer road on the other side of the gate.

Stefan heard the clip-clop of the horse, before he saw the carriage come into view. Katya, Alexie and Sofie were returning from Zagreb.

Stefan rose, brushing off the dog hairs from his trousers as he walked toward the approaching carriage. He couldn't make out the expressions on their faces. He hoped they were not bringing back bad news.

Katya stood in the carriage and waved furiously at Stefan. "Stefan…Stefan." She called his name excitedly.

From the road, seeing Katya waving frantically, Ivan moved faster. Everyone knew that Teta Sofie had gone to see the well-known Dr. Popovich in Zagreb.

Ivan caught up to Stefan and the two stood anxiously waiting, as Alexie, Sofie and Katya, descended from the carriage. Confused, the half-brothers watched as Katya and Sofie were laughing or crying or possibly doing both.

CHAPTER 14

In the house, Klara and Anton, cried, hugged and kissed Sofie. They couldn't hug her close enough or kiss her enough times. Stefan and Ivan smiled awkwardly, not knowing how to react to the news.

Alexie took his beloved, Sofie, by the hand and seated her at the dining table. Her eyes were swollen and red from crying. She smoothed the skirt of her brown shirt waist dress. Her hands trembled slightly. Alexie, with his hands on her shoulders, stood protectively behind her chair.

Zora, the cook, standing at the kitchen door, babushka on her head, a flour dusted apron over her skirt, thought she would wet herself with excitement. Here she was with the most fantastic news ever and she couldn't leave to tell anyone.

Klara sat on the chair next to Sofie. "Is it true? Could he be wrong?" she demanded. "Doctors can be wrong."

Alexie spoke, "Dr. Popovich is confident that Sofie is three months pregnant!"

Anton spoke up concerned. "Will she be alright? Why has she been so ill?"

Alexie explained, "There are women who may be ill throughout their entire pregnancies and he believes Sofie is one of these women."

During his examination of Sofie, Dr. Popovich had every reason to believe she had at some time given birth. He said nothing to Alexie or Sofie, for they both did not mention it. It seemed to him they did not want to talk about it. It was a strange visit, the doctor thought. A woman who had a baby once, surely knew the signs of pregnancy the second time. And yet, Sofie confided her fear to the doctor that she was dying.

Sofie took Klara's hand, saying, "Can you believe it? You will be a Kuma to our child. I want you to be our child's Godmother."

Tears streamed down the old friend's cheeks. "At your age, you must be careful." she said.

"She is not that old." said her brother Anton. "She isn't forty, yet. Many women in the village still have children at this age."

Ivan stepped forward and took Teta Sofie's hand. He kissed it and said, "I am so happy for you both. I can't wait to tell my parents." He moved back, careful not to step awkwardly on anyone's foot or accidently bump them with his cane.

Stefan knelt before his aunt. "This is wonderful news." he said. "But, you must be careful. We want you and the baby to be fine." He kissed her on each cheek.

Both Ivan and Stefan stood in the back ground, feeling somewhat awkward. This baby stuff was for women. Men never quite know what to say or do.

The two of them stepped out into the warm sunlight, to have a smoke.

"I see you have dog." laughed Ivan. He had already heard how the dog wanted to be with Stefan.

Offering Ivan a cigarette, Stefan looked long at Pas, who was at his side. "I can't explain it. He thinks he is mine."

"Any idea where he came from?" Ivan pulled a match from his pocket.

"None at all. He just appeared when Father Mika came to drop off some books that Lahdra wanted Ta to have." Stefan patted Pas on the head.

"Did he come with Father Mika?"

"I don't think so." said, Stefan. "Pas was already here, when the priest arrived."

Ivan laughed when he heard "Pas."

"Is that it? You are going to call him Pas? Just, Dog? Not very original."

"I don't know. I can't think of anything that fits him." Stefan smiled at the big animal. "I must admit, I do like him."

Katya, wearing a long-sleeved, straight white dress, with white satin trim came towards them. She was stunning in the Italian dress, looking every bit the sophisticated lady. Her copper hair sparkled in the sunlight.

Both men rose, as she neared and made room for her to sit in between them.

"I came for a cigarette." she said, smiling at the look of surprise on both their faces. "Oh, come now," she continued, "I have been smoking for a long time. It is quite acceptable, you know."

Stefan offered her an Italian cigarette, then held a match for her.

"Do you like these?" she asked, meaning the cigarettes.

"No, I prefer the Turkish ones." answered Stefan.

"So do I." she said.

Ivan couldn't help staring at her. She was his Katya and yet, she wasn't. He missed the peasant girl he remembered. The sight of this sophisticated, continental woman still stirred something deep within him, but the Katya who appeared at his brother's wedding two years ago, was gone. He watched her closely as she and Stefan talked about cigarettes, food and places he had never heard of.

He listened as they spoke, but didn't hear what they were saying. He kept wondering what had happened to his Katya. His beloved Katya, who once wore her hair loose and wild like a Gypsy.

Her face seemed slimmer, her cheekbones a little more prominent. Her green eyes still sparkled, but now looked at the world with assurance, not with the shyness he remembered. He noticed that she sat with her ankles crossed primly. Her fingernails had a shine to them. She sat with her back straight. The only thing that reminded him of the old Katya, was the bracelet that peaked out from under her long sleeve when she lifted the cigarette to her lips.

It was the bracelet that was to protect her from danger. The bracelet the Gypsy Queen, Valina had given her. And…it had protected her from danger. It was when the Gypsy, Mustafa, saw the bracelet that he plunged his knife into the back of the Turk.

Ivan was so overtaken by a wave of sadness that he rose, flinging his cigarette to the ground.

"I…I must leave." he said. "I need to go home."

He didn't look at Stefan or Katya because he had tears in his eyes. He had been longing for a girl that no longer existed for him. He had dreamt of her and wished for her return every day for two years and now she was here. But, it wasn't Katya. She had become someone else. He wished he would never have to see her again. For him, the pain of the loss that he now accepted choked him. The Katya of two years ago, no longer existed.

CHAPTER 15

That evening Sofie sat at the dining table for dinner instead of eating in her room. She felt tired, but far too happy to spend any more time upstairs in bed. *She was going to be a mother.* The words kept running through her mind.

Alexie beamed with pride. A smile was permanently fixed on his face. He hoped Sofie would give him a boy, but he would be happy with a daughter. However, a boy could run the trading company in Trieste better than a girl, he thought.

Klara was so happy one would have thought she was going to be the mother. "I am going to get some yarn and start making baby things." she announced proudly.

Anton was happy, but pensive. His sister did not have a grave illness, for that he would give God thanks. Instead she was going to have a baby, an addition to the family. Deep in his heart he was sad that she now lived in Trieste. How he wished he could watch the baby grow and be a real part of the household! Instead, the child would possibly grow to be a stranger, visiting only occasionally. The thought depressed him.

He said to Sofie, "Have you thought of having the baby here, in your home?"

Before she could answer, Alexie said, "Her home is now in Trieste."

"I wonder," said Sofie, thoughtfully, "perhaps I should have the baby here. Here with Klara, and all my family and friends."

"You have family and friends in Trieste." Alexie's voice was low. "I would want to be with you when the baby is born."

The conversation halted as Zora brought in a platter of potato pancakes. She placed the pancakes on the center of the floral embroidered tablecloth and returned to the kitchen for the fried apples to serve with the pancakes.

Anton nodded for Alexie to serve himself and Sofie. He passed a plate to Katya who took one of the crisply fried cakes.

Klara left the table going to the kitchen to find the large sugar shaker. She liked to sprinkle sugar on the pancakes. Actually, she liked to sprinkle sugar on almost everything.

To change the subject, Stefan said, "Father Mika was here this morning."

"Really?" Sofie, said, "I haven't met him." "Why was he here?"

Returning from the kitchen, Klara placed the sugar shaker on the table. She said, "He brought some books for Anton. Books Lahdra had wanted Anton to have."

"Why do you suppose he wanted to give you books?" Sofie looked at Anton. "Was he returning the ones you gave him over the years?"

Anton didn't answer.

Stefan said, "These appear to be his ledgers, his personal diaries."

Sofie's eyes grew large. She looked to her brother. "Have you looked at them?"

Anton put down his fork, took a sip of their homemade wine. "I don't think I can. Not yet."

"Would you mind if I looked through them?" asked, Stefan. "Or, would I be intruding?"

"If you wish." said his father. "I can't bring myself to look at them."

It had been a pleasant evening, quiet and enjoyable. There was talk about the baby and how Sofie should rest and be careful during her pregnancy. The only jarring note had been Anton's suggestion that Sofie have the baby at Vladezemla. The thought of Sofie staying in Vladezemla made Anton uncomfortable. He wasn't sure why he felt that way. Trieste had become home for him and he liked running the trading company. He was especially fond of Seniora Kurecka, who had inherited the company from her father and now gave it to Sofie and Alexie. It did not bother Alexie that she had been Vincent's mother or even that Sofie had once loved Vincent. Sofie was his now and so was the Renaldi Trading Company.

The meal finished, Katya excused herself going to her old room close to the attic. Alexie and Sofie were staying on the second floor where Sofie's room remained as it had been when she left for Trieste.

Downstairs Klara dozed in a large comfortable chair, snoring softly every now and then. Anton went out to smoke and make his nightly visit to the comfort of the chapel.

With his huge paw, Pas pulled the door open and sneaked into the house. Pas went directly to where Stefan sat in the parlor. Lahdra's ledgers were stacked on the floor beside Stefan's chair. Pas laid his head next to Stefan's feet.

The books ranged from his early ones, written on paper covered notebooks to the later leather covered books. Stefan pulled out a red ribbon obviously marking a special page in one of the leather books. He read the page marked with the ribbon and several pages after it. As Stefan read, he became aware that his heart was beating faster. As he turned each page, he noticed a very slight trembling of his hands as he read. He glanced at Klara, but she was asleep in the chair near him.

What Stefan read was terribly important and hard to believe. If it had not been written by Lahdra's own hand, Stefan would not have believed it.

With the ledger in his hand, he rose and said, "Aide, come, Pas." The dog followed Stefan to the door and went out into the night to sleep on the porch.

Taking the ledger with him, Stefan, feeling tears in his eyes, climbed the stairs to his own room. He was weak with emotion. Morning was soon enough to read the passages to the family

CHAPTER 16

An unhappy and confused Zora walked down the sloping road leading to her small wooden home. She had arrived to work on time. She put her walking shoes on a low shelf, and slipped on soft household slippers. Before she had time to get the flour and eggs to start the morning meal, Klara was there to tell her she could go home. Puzzled, the lanky cook asked, "Zashto? Why? Am I being dismissed? Have I displeased Gospodine Vladislav in some way?" Thoughts raced through her mind. Did they know she was carrying gossip back to the village? Was that it? Boze Moj! Dear God, she was sure she was being fired.

"No, no. Not at all." said Klara, patting Zora's thin arm. She handed Zora a sack of apples. "You just go home and enjoy your day. Make some strudel for the family with these apples."

"Have I done something?" She asked again, "Something to make you angry?" The tall woman didn't want to lose her status as the cook to the Vladeslavs. She was quite popular with the villagers who were always hungry for gossip about the most important family in the area.

"No, no..." soothed Klara. "We just want you to have a day to yourself."

Zora tried to think what she could have done to make them ask her to go home. When she first arrived that morning she was aware of some whispering in the dining room between the Gospodine, Klara and Stefan.

There was something big going on and she didn't have a clue what it could be. Going home would definitely cut into her daily dispensing of gossip. Ever since Stefan came home, her popularity in the village had grown. Every evening on her way home, her neighbors waited along the road to hear what was going on with Stefan, or the red haired witch.

"Do you see her casting spells?" someone would ask. "Don't look her in the eyes...that's when she will give you the evil eye." warned another.

The word that Sofie was pregnant really titillated the villagers. The fact that old maid, Teta Sofie, beloved though she was, found a

65

husband had been news enough. And now...she was pregnant! Of course, they were happy for her, but this was news! With no radio and only an occasional outdated newspaper, which most of them could not read, any gossip was eagerly awaited, accepted and spread with the speed and fury of a fierce storm.

With no explanation of why Zora was sent home, her neighbors would speculate for a reason. After all, what else did they have to do, but talk about one another?

Sitting at the table, drinking the morning coffee which Zora had started and Klara completed, Stefan was disappointed to see his father once again dressed in home spun loose trousers and shirt. His once gleaming beautiful boots were now replaced with opanke, the leather footwear made in the villages.

"Why are you being so secretive? Why can't you tell us why we had to send Zora away?" asked an annoyed Anton, sitting in his chair at the head of the table. He nodded a 'good morning' to Klara seated next to him.

"I want us to all be together when I disclose what I have discovered." said, Stefan. "I don't want to go over it more than once."

Anton looked at Stefan. "You are being mysterious." he said as he noticed Katya coming down the stairs, dressed in her favorite green full skirt and scoop necked blouse. Her red hair was coiled neatly in a bun at the nape of her slender neck. She said, "Dorbo Yutro, Good morning" and sat at her place at the table which was now next to Stefan.

"Dobro Yutro," replied Klara and Anton. Stefan stared at Katya as if he were seeing her for the first time.

Katya seated next to Stefan, noticing his stare asked, "Is something the matter? Why are you looking at me that way?"

"No...nothing." he stammered. "I'm sorry, I didn't mean to stare."

Klara and Anton looked from Katya to Stefan. Then at one another, clearly there was something wrong.

Stefan stole glances at Katya, wishing not to stare, but looking for something in her face, something he may have missed.

What *was* missing was not with Katya, but the usual morning conversations. Today there was no small talk and no Zora coming and going from the kitchen.

"Where is Zora?" Katya looked toward the kitchen. "Is she ill?"

"Ask Stefan." said Klara, with a wave of her hand. "He wanted her sent away."

They all turned to the stairway hearing Alexie and Sofie coming down. Sofie wore a blue dressing gown and Alexie was fully dressed. Sofie was pale, but now that she knew she was to have a baby instead of a terrible illness, she refused to stay upstairs wanting to be with the family.

"Come and sit." said, Klara. "We are all anxious to know what Stefan wants to tell us." Then she added, "And why he had me send Zora away."

Alexie motioned for Klara to stay seated while he poured coffee for Sofie and himself.

"This appears to be a family meeting." said Anton, feeling some tension in the air.

Missing from the table were the usual fragrant home baked bread or rolls.

Seeing everyone with full coffee cups, Anton turned to his son, "Alright Stefan," he said. "We are all here. Now tell us what is so important."

Stefan looked around the table at each of them. He wasn't sure how to present what he found in Lahdra's diary. Should he read directly from the pages, or just tell them what he found?

From his lap, Stefan lifted the ledger and placed it on the table.

Seeing the book and feeling the painful loss of his best friend, Anton started to rise. "I am not ready for this." His voice was hoarse.

Stefan grabbed his father's arm, holding him. "Ta...this is important." Stefan looked around the table at the startled faces. "You have no idea how important this is." he said gravely.

Anton lowered himself into his chair. Saying nothing he placed his two hands flat on the table, one on each side of his coffee cup. The others looked on in silent anticipation.

"Well…" started Stefan. "As I remember, Father Lahdra had been the priest in the village where Katya…where…" He started to say was born, but stopped. Instead he said, "Katya came from."

Sitting next to Stefan, Katya turned to look him full in the face. Her eyes wide with wonder. *What did this have to do with her?*

Before anyone could speak, Stefan continued. "Lahdra did remember the people who raised Katya."

Still staring at Stefan, now with a wary look, Katya said, "You mean my family."

Anton, Klara, Sofie and Alexie all remained silent looking intently at Stefan and Katya. No one touched the coffee before them. Some instinct within each of them kept them from speaking.

Stefan nervously looked around the table. Feeling Katya's eyes on his face he said "Now I will read from the ledger."

They all watched as Stefan removed the red ribbon from the book which marked a page.

He read the words written by Father Lahdra:

'My hand trembles as I put these words down, here, in my most secret of places. So much has happened in the last thirty-six hours. It is breaking my heart and makes me wonder how I can go on, being burdened as I am.

A man attempted to kill my dearest friend Anton. Instead, the killer was killed. Ernesta and Ivan were attacked, perhaps by different persons or the same.'

Here, Stefan's voice choked as he went on,

'Stefan has disappeared. Did he know of these events?

We sat through the night watching Katya tend Ivan's wounds. I held my rosary throughout the night. So much of what I witnessed may have been witchcraft.'

The look of disgust on Katya's face did not go unnoticed by the others as Stefan continued reading.

'Early in the morning, upon my return from the all night vigil at the Balaban house, I found that I was summoned to the convent. My cousin, Manda, the Mother Superior needed me.

Tears fall on these pages as I write. Those last few hours with Anton, Ivan and Manda have been so painful.

Manda was dying. She did die. My vigil with Ivan was made with loving friends, while my vigil with Manda was made alone and with great emotional pain. I heard Manda's last confession, stayed with her through the night and when the nuns awoke me in the morning, she was gone. Her soul had left.

Now…here is where I have my greatest inner struggle. The laws of the Church forbid me from revealing what I have heard in confession. And yet, if it means hellfire and damnation, I am compelled to reveal what I know. This truth must be told.

Manda confessed that on the day, so long ago, when I came to the convent and first met Anton, Sofie had been brought there very ill. Anton thought Sofie was dying. She was not dying, she was pregnant.'

"That can't be!" Sofie cried out interrupting the reading. She struggled to stand, knocking over her coffee, spilling it on the red tablecloth. There was commotion as Klara tried to get up to help clean the spilled coffee, but Katya was already in the kitchen getting towels.

Still in shock at the statement, Sofie shouted at Anton. "Anton you were there. This can't be true." She was sobbing while a bewildered Alexie wrapped a comforting arm around her shoulders.

Anton ran to her side taking her hand, "No one said anything about a baby. Of course it can't be true."

Klara at her seat kept repeating, "O Boze Moy and Sveta Maika Boze. O Dear God and Holy Mother of God."

Katya brought towels for the spilled coffee. Alexie took an extra towel to wipe Sofie's tear stained face.

Stefan said in a low calm voice, "There is much more. I must go on."

Alexie helped Sofie in her chair and sat down himself. Alexie asked, "Should we go on. This seems to be disturbing to us all."

Gravely, Stefan said, "I must go on."

69

All eyes were on Stefan. What more could there be? Would there be more upsetting revelations? A quiet uneasiness awaited the continued reading.

Stefan continued and Sofie moaned aloud when she heard,

'Sister Filippa pressed on Sofie's stomach to force the baby out. Seeing the baby not breathing, Manda took it to the garden along the convent wall where she buried it.

Manda kept this a secret from Anton because she feared the family would no longer support the convent.'

Hearing this, Anton cradled his head with both hands saying, "Sveti Isus! Holy Jesus."

With the tiniest bit of jealousy, Alexie asked Sofie, "This was Vincent's baby?"

Sofie dropped her head, hiding them in her hands. "A yoy, a yoy." She wailed.

From some mysterious place a rosary had appeared in Klara's plump fingers.

A sad Anton was remembering that trip in the open carriage from Trieste when he was ordered by their father to bring Sofie home. Vincent had just died and Anton refused to stay for the funeral, taking an angry, crying Sofie home with him. She was so very ill in the carriage, that he feared she was dying of the same disease that had taken Vincent's life. Anton remembered she was lying on the floor of the carriage instead of sitting in the seat. *Oh, dear God. He had been so mean to her on that journey!*

"Teta Sofie," Stefan said softly, "I must go on."

Katya stood and nearly shouted at Stefan, "What more can there be? Look what you have done to Teta Sofie! Is this necessary?"

Katya felt a chill when Stefan looked her in the eyes and said, "Oh, yes, Katya. It is more necessary than you could ever guess."

Katya slowly sat down. Deep inside, she felt something was not right.

Stefan read more from the ledger,

'Upon leaving Manda's cell, Sister Filippa approached me. She wanted me to hear her confession. I was weary and emotionally worn, so I tried to refuse. She insisted.

She also told me of the baby and that Manda had buried it. Fearing the baby would go to limbo, for it had not been baptized. Sister Filippa removed the baby from its very shallow grave.

She said that at that very moment a crazed man leaped from the wall, demanding a baby. He threw money at her and told her it was his Amerika money and that he needed to bring a baby to his Mila. For all these years Sister Filippa has felt guilt for giving him the baby which she thought to be dead.

I am so tortured! Because this information came to me in the sacrament of confession, I cannot tell Sofie and Anton the truth about that baby. The baby was taken to Selna. A pregnant mother was buried with her own dead baby in her body. Everyone thought the living baby was a twin of the unborn baby. Everyone knew that Mato had been saving money for Amerika! His wife's name was Mila!

I know that the baby taken to Selna and raised as Katya Balich is Sofie's child.'

No one had heard Zora when she came back into the kitchen. In Klara's rush to send her home, Zora forgot her shoes. She quietly opened the kitchen door and pulled off her slippers. She heard crying and loud voices. Curiosity led her to the slightly opened dining room door.

She stayed just long enough to hear that Sofie Vladeslav Lukas had a baby out of wedlock…and that the baby was now the red-haired witch!

CHAPTER 17

Ivan walked slowly up the inclined road to Vladezemla. He no longer felt the need to be there early each morning. In fact, now that Stefan was back, Ivan felt it would only be a matter of time when Stefan would be in charge.

He didn't really care. It was his mother, Vera, who wanted Vladezemla to be Ivan's. To Ivan, this land was a symbol of his mother's youthful love of Anton. In Ivan's mind, the stocky, blacksmith, Marko Balaban was his true father. He still thought of Anton as his Kum, his Godfather. Ivan's respect and affection for his step father, Marko, grew stronger with the passing of time. His father carried himself with dignity even in the face of rude or sarcastic remarks from their neighbors when it became known that Anton had fathered Ivan instead of Marko. As time passed, the remarks were less and less, but Ivan knew his neighbors still talked about them.

Coming down the road, at almost a full run, Ivan recognized Zora, the cook. "What's wrong?" He grabbed her arm, stopping her. "Has something happened?"

Zora raised her hands to heaven and kept repeating, "Boze Moi, Boze Moi. My God, My God."

"Zora, stop it. What is wrong? What has happened?" he demanded, fearing the worst.

"Oh, Mother of God," she wailed, "Gospa Sofie is Katya's mother."

"Of course she is." said, Ivan. "Teta Sofie adopted her long ago."

"No! No!" Zora was almost giddy. She was hopping up and down.

"Sofie Vladeslav had a baby at the convent and she wasn't married. The nuns kept the baby."

Zora wasn't sure if the look on Ivan's face was one of anger or disgust. Suddenly she realized she had said too much. She knew she was in big trouble. She should have kept still…kept her mouth shut. Of all the people to blab to, she did it to Ivan who was by birth, a Vladeslav.

"Come back here, Zora." demanded Ivan, as she ran down the road, not only to her home, but to spread this fantastic secret.

On the porch of Anton's house, Pas greeted Ivan and was rewarded with a pat on the head.

Ivan didn't knock. He opened the door when he heard the crying and loud voices.

There was Katya in Sofie's arms and both of them sobbing wildly. Klara had her hands to her face and she too, was sobbing. Anton still seated at the head of the table, looked as if he had been slapped. Stefan with the ledger before him on the table just looked on, not knowing what would happen next.

Alexie, strong, calm Alexie, leaned against the wall. This news, this revelation should change nothing in his and Sofie's life...yet, deep inside he wondered if it would.

"Is it true?" Ivan asked. Everyone looked up surprised at Ivan's appearance. "Is it true that Katya is really our cousin?"

Stefan rose reaching a hand to Ivan. "Come sit down." He pulled out a chair for Ivan. "How do you know about this? We only found out this morning."

"Zora met me on the road. She was hurrying home. She told me." Ivan saw the looks of dismay on all their faces knowing that soon she would tell everyone. He stretched his bad leg out and settled in the chair.

Klara swore, "Jeba, Zora." It was the only time any of them had ever heard Klara use that word.

Sofie was in her chair and Katya on the floor before her, her head in Sofie's lap. There were still tears, but the great sobbing had subsided. Sofie caressed Katya's hair.

"Can it be true?" asked Katya, in between sobs.

"Alexie..." Sofie motioned for him to come close. "Go to our room. In the bottom drawer of the small chest, under the nightgowns is a small picture. Please bring it to me."

Alexie found the picture and it saddened him. It had to be a miniature portrait of Vincent, he was certain. As he made his way downstairs he tried to convince himself that Vincent was so very long ago and has been long dead. Sofie was his wife, now. Alexie never doubted Sofie's love for a moment. But…long gone feelings may be stirring.

Alexie handed the small oval painted portrait to Sofie. While she looked at it, Alexie wondered what Sofie was thinking and feeling.

Sofie remembered looking at this picture that very first night when she met Katya at Nikola Balaban's wedding to young Luba. It was Katya's red hair that made Sofie look at the portrait and see Vincent's red hair. She handed the picture to Katya.

Katya wiped the tears from her eyes with the sleeve of her blouse, bumping her cheek slightly with the amulet bracelet.

Katya stared at the small oval picture of a young man with red hair. As she looked at it, she couldn't help but think with longer hair, it could be a picture of her. In a hushed voice, she said, "I think it looks like me."

Stefan and Ivan both leaned over Katya for a look and they had to agree, she did indeed resemble the portrait.

Even Klara came to look at the picture. As she nodded, she said, "Yoy mene…Oh, my."

Anton remained in his chair remembering the dying Vincent with his horribly thin body, grey skin and the foul odor in the sick room. "Get the slivovica." he said, "We all need something stronger than this cold coffee."

Klara found some hard cheese and yesterday's bread, which she brought out and set on the table. She also set down a stack of plates and some knives.　They had to eat something. Still, this wasn't enough. Back in the kitchen she found some apples and brought them out.

"What now?" asked Ivan.

"Nothing has changed." said Alexie. He cut a piece of cheese and gave it to Sofie. "Katya was adopted and treated like a daughter. Now, we know she *is* the daughter and everything should remain the same.

Sofie said to everyone, "I knew from the moment I met Katya that I needed her near me." She patted Katya's hand, "Destiny brought you to me."

Concerned about his wife, Alexie said, "Sofie, you have had a lot of excitement. Should you lie down?"

"Not yet." she said. 'I am feeling calmer now. Perhaps it is the slivovica or just the comfort of knowing the truth. We are truly a family now. All of us." She reached out, took Ivan's hand and smiled at him. He was more than a Godson to her. He was Anton's son and her bratich...her nephew.

To her brother she said, "Look at us, Anton. Do you feel the great gift Lahdra has given us?"

Anton sighed heavily, "I see more gossip, more jokes and laughter behind our backs."

"We got through all of that before." said Ivan referring to the gossip, when it was revealed that Anton was his father. "I don't care what anyone says. I am pleased for Teta Sofie and for Katya."

Klara spoke up. "Well, I guess it is back into the kitchen for me. If ever I see that Zora again I'll hit her with a broom."

"While we are here, I can help you in the kitchen." said, Katya. "We will get along without Zora."

Later after Alexie helped Sofie up to her bed and Katya went to stay with her, he returned to sit with Stefan and Ivan. Anton went out for a smoke and his daily visit to the chapel where he felt at peace praying.

Ivan was comfortable sitting with Stefan. Neither felt any of the tension of their youth. Stefan no longer resented Ivan or thought Ivan his father's favorite. In fact, now, he felt something he sensed might be brotherly affection. He even thought to find a foot stool for Ivan's damaged leg.

To Alexie, who had been an advokat before moving to Trieste, Stefan said, "I would like you to read something. Do you mind?"

"Of course not," said Alexie.

From his jacket pocket, Stefan pulled out a folded piece of paper. Leaning forward he passed the paper to Alexie.

Before Alexie unfolded the paper, Stefan said, "Please tell me what you think."

The look on Alexie's face showed mild surprise. Then there was a small smile. "Well, I think this is legal, if that is what you want to know."

"That's what I want to know." admitted Stefan.

A confused Ivan looked from Alexie to Stefan.

Alexie returned the paper to Stefan, who handed it to Ivan, who read it and asked, "Is this true?"

Alexie said, "It has to be true. That paper is Magda's last will. She left all her possessions to Stefan. She never sold her establishment to the Turk and he is dead. So…I think Stefan might be the owner of a gambling house and brothel in Zagreb."

Klara, carrying plates hearing the conversation from the kitchen doorway, cried out, "Sveta Maria…Holy Mary!" Then she dropped the dishes.

CHAPTER 18

It was different this time. There was no laughter, no open ridicule of Sofie, no snickering or finger pointing. There was an unusual quiet in the valley.

Yes, this was different...very different.

Sofie was the mother of a witch. Even the strong-hearted men who had laughed at their superstitious wives, were not taking any chances. After all, Katya was known to be a witch and protected by the Queen Valina. Everyone knew that Gypsies could cast spells.

"What about that bracelet she always wears?" They wondered aloud. "The one with all those jewels and strange designs, it could be magical."

Zora was the most frightened of all. She did not return to her work at the Vladeslav kitchen, nor did she want to retrieve her house slippers. No doubt there was already a curse on them and who knew what would happen to her when she placed them on her feet. No, she wasn't taking any chances. She would crochet new slippers.

The talk of Sofie having a baby at the convent and the baby being Katya and Katya's mysterious arrival at the Balaban wedding were certainly discussed, but, in hushed voices or whispers.

Leaving Vladezemla on his way home, Ivan expected taunts or jeers during his walk. Instead those he passed on the road averted his eyes or turned away from him. After all...he was the witch's cousin.

Anton had not traveled in all the time that Stefan was gone or while Ernesta was ill. His arranged marriage never developed the love that often comes with time. Perhaps if Vera had not been so close, and Ivan a constant reminder of their youthful love...he might have made it work with Ernesta.

Anton had become a recluse of sorts. He spent his time reading and going to his lovely little chapel to pray.

It took Stefan a good deal of talking to convince his father to go to Zagreb with him to see what Magda had left him in her will. Anton came up with every excuse he could think of to refuse. Most of all,

Anton was not at all pleased to hear his son may be the owner of a gambling house.

"Please, Tata," urged Stefan, "I need your advice. I know nothing about property or what to do with it."

"If you are planning on opening up Magda's as it was, I want no part of it." growled Anton. "We can't have our name connected with a brothel."

So now, two days after Stefan read Father Lahdra's journals, he and Anton were in sunny Zagreb seated at an outdoor kafana. It was late morning and both men looked quite good dressed in suits and tasteful cravats. Anton's clothing was not cut as stylish as Stefan's, but he looked marvelous in his dark brown suit. Stefan was delighted to see his father once again looking almost elegant.

In the past two years, some grey found its way to Anton's temples and his moustache was not quite as dark, never the less he was still a handsome man.

Anton did in fact, enjoy being with his son. The carriage ride into Zagreb was pleasant. But, being a stubborn man, Anton was not yet ready to forgive Stefan entirely for being gone two years and for traveling with a madam.

"How long are we to wait?" asked Anton. "I thought we were to meet an attorney." Then he added, "Why does he have to go with us?"

"Alexie suggested it." said Stefan. "Enjoy the nice breeze, look at all the people."

There was much activity in the square. It was market day with villagers in every sort of colorful clothing. A young man leading a goat with a rope walked past them. He wore form fitting black trousers, a white shirt laced with cord and over the shirt a black vest. The vest was embroidered with red and white scrolls. On his feet were leather opanke, shoes with the toes curled upward.

Nearby a pretty woman dressed in a homespun skirt and matching blouse with red designs embroidered on her sleeves, was selling handmade laces. Her thick red apron had coins sewn onto it as decoration. Her necklace was also made of coins. The little girl with her was also dressed in white, wearing only a simple red apron. The girl had a basket of flowers to sell.

The air was fragrant with the smell of flowers and the aroma of chivapcici sausages cooking somewhere in the square. Musicians walked about playing tamburitza music, accepting folded money slipped under the instrument's strings for a special request.

Tourists in all sorts of European clothing were walking about the market, looking at the variety of offerings for sale.

A man's voice called out, "Stefan! Stefan Vladeslav is that you?"

Stefan and Anton both turned, their eyes following the sound of the voice. Stefan spotted the man hurrying towards them and rose to greet him.

"My goodness! Stefan where have you been?" A short, balding man, with a round belly, asked as he extended his hand in greeting. "We haven't seen you or the Contessa in ages." The man then politely turned and made a formal bow to Anton.

"Giorgio, may I present my father, Anton Vladeslav." To his father he said, "Giorgio Palma, a friend from Italy."

Anton was very impressed by Giorgio Palma. By his dress and demeanor it was obvious this was an educated and wealthy man. "Won't you join us?" Anton offered.

"Thank you, but I must decline." He rolled his eyes, "I can't keep the Princess waiting."

"We understand," said Stefan, "another time."

As Giorgio hurried off towards the Palace Hotel at Strossmayer Square he gave a final wave to Stefan.

"How do you know that man?" asked Anton.

"We met often in our travels and sometimes played cards." said Stefan, his attention drawn to a 1902 Fiat as it slowly made its way through the crowded street. Stefan was not the only one looking at the auto. It was an open car with large brass lamps on the front. The seats were bright red tufted leather. Curious onlookers stood dangerously in the middle of the street for a better look.

"This is the first automobile I have seen since I left Italy." he said.

"I am not sure those things are safe." said Anton. "Now, tell me about that Palma man."

"Oh, Giorgio is pleasant enough. Not a very good card player." Stefan paused a moment, delighting in what he was about to say. "He is related to Princess Elena de Savoy of Italy."

The stunned look on Anton's face pleased Stefan, though he tried to hide it. Anton stared at his son for several moments. He said, "You know such people?"

"Yes, Ta, Magda and I were very lucky in the people we met."

"This Magda," wondered Anton aloud, "Is she the one Palma referred to as contessa? Why would he call her that?"

"Ta," Stefan started to explain, "We never used the title of count or contessa." Seeing the look of disapproval on Anton's face, Stefan said, "It was because of how we dressed and behaved that people assumed we were…were, better than we really were."

Tired of waiting for the advokat, who never appeared, Stefan and Anton took the short walk to the stone building only a block away, that was once Magda's. The large house had been where one gambled downstairs and could be entertained with lovely young women and girls upstairs.

To Stefan's surprise, the yard inside the gate looked better than he had expected. There were no flowers in the stone planters and he saw that the windows were shuttered. He pulled a key from his pants pocket and inserted it in the ornate brass lock. When it wouldn't turn, Anton asked, "Is that the right key?"

With some giggling and a hard turn, the lock opened. The hinges squealed as Stefan pushed open the door. He stepped back so his father could enter first.

The large room smelled of musty old wood and dust. Dust particles sparkled and danced in the streams of sunlight that found their way through the slats of the shuttered windows. The baccarat table and the side gaming tables were just as Magda had left them.

Now, after two years of being uncovered, a dusty grey film covered everything.

Anton said, "Well, we know we can't sit anywhere. Look at all this dust."

The building had once been a grand house. The main floor may have been a ballroom, common in Victorian mansions. A great staircase at one wall lead to what had been the living quarters upstairs, later turned into the brothel.

Stefan moved away from his father towards a door. In the dim light, Anton demanded, "Where are you going?"

Stefan laughed. "Are you frightened? No one is here. Only we are here."

Just then, a man's voice boomed from the far side of the room. "Who are you? What are you doing here?" In the gloom, he was hard to see.

"I am the owner and who are you?" called back Stefan.

"You aren't the owner." The voice replied. "I know the owner and you are not Magda."

Stefan moved quickly toward the sound of the voice. "I have the key." Stefan said sternly, "What are you doing here and how did you get in?"

When Stefan was close, he could see that the man looked old and very thin. His face was gaunt. His straggly mustache matched his yellowish gray hair. His clothing was that of a worker…brown loose trousers, with a pullover shirt of some heavy brown material.

"Who are you?" Stefan asked again.

With Anton close beside Stefan, the old man felt intimated. He said, "I am Ignatz, the caretaker."

Stefan studied the old man and said, "Magda never mentioned a caretaker. And," he added, "I don't remember seeing you here."

The old man sank into a dusty chair, tears in his eyes. "She used to give me food every night. She was such a good woman."

He pulled the tail of his shirt to wipe the tears that welled in his eyes. "When she didn't open one day, I thought something happened to her." Ignatz looked at Stefan and Anton not sure what the future held for him. Would he be put in jail? He hurried on to explain, "On the second day, after the girls couldn't get in. You know…the girls who worked upstairs. I waited till they were gone and I forced the lock on the back door."

Ignatz waited for Stefan or Anton to say something. When they remained silent, he went on. "So, I waited. I found a little food. When people came and knocked at the door to come in, I hid. After awhile people stopped coming."

"How have you lived?" asked Anton.

Not so afraid, now, the old man continued. "After some time, I started to sleep in the back. Back where Magda lived. I thought it would be alright because I was taking care of things for her. I watched that no one came in. I would find work once in awhile for money."

"Stay there." Stefan ordered Ignatz in a firm voice.

Anton and Stefan walked away towards the front of the room, so the frightened man could not hear them.

"What do you think, Ta?" asked Stefan. "Should I let him stay on and watch the place?"

Anton felt pity for the man. He could see the tears on Ignatz's cheeks and said, "He appears harmless and honest."

"Good! I was thinking the same." said Stefan.

When Anton and Stefan approached Ignatz, he rose from the chair waiting for them to speak. He was sure they would turn him out, or worse, have him put in prison.

Stefan asked, "Would you like to stay here?" Before the man could answer Stefan said, "Magda died and I am the new, Gazda, boss."

Ignatz was surprised to hear Magda was dead and quickly made the sign of the cross. "She was a good woman. She gave me food." he said again.

"Listen," said Stefan, "I want you to stay here, just as you have."

Because Croatia was under the rule of Austria-Hungary, the bills Stefan took from his pocket were Austrian krone bank notes. He handed them to Ignatz.

"Take this money and buy food and some new clothes." Stefan said, "You work for me, now."

A stunned Ignatz stared at the money as if it were not real. He looked from Stefan to the smiling Anton, who was pleased with what Stefan had done.

Ignatz fell to his knees, taking Stefan's hand, he kissed it in gratitude.

"No, no…none of that." Stefan was embarrassed.

"Mnogo, mnogo hvala…many, many thanks." Ignatz was still on his knees.

"Now, get up. Don't carry on so." Stefan helped Ignatz up. "I'll be here tomorrow and we can look around and decide what should be done."

Clutching the krone notes to his chest, a shocked Ignatz his eyes wide with wonder, could only nod in agreement.

Stefan smiled when he saw the pleased and proud look on his father's face.

"Well, now," said Stefan, "let's look around."

He went to the office which was to the left of the entry door. It was the room, two years ago, where he met the awful Turk, Magda's new business partner. Stefan felt a shiver run though him, as he remembered that awful encounter. He had been given one week to pay his debt or the debt would be doubled.

At the door, he slowly turned the handle and pushed it open. He stepped inside. The room smelled musty and was dark. Stefan went to the windows and pulled open the heavy velvet drapes releasing a shower of dust.

He looked around the room. Then…in an awed whisper he said,

"Sveti Isus e Mayka Boze…Holy Jesus and Blessed Mother of God.

CHAPTER 19

The following morning, an excited Anton returned alone to Vladezemla.

He told the family about the trip to Zagreb, meeting Giorgio Palma, a cousin of the Princess Elena of Italy, of Ignatz the self-appointed caretaker and lastly of what he and Stefan saw in the office. Hearing of the building and the contents of the office, Sofie insisted her beloved Alexie leave immediately for Zagreb.

Alexie had no thought of going to Zagreb. His concern was for Sofie. He certainly hadn't planned on having company on this trip. He had no choice. The day before Pas, the dog, had spent the entire day and night lying in the middle of the road facing the direction Stefan and Anton took when they left for Zagreb. As if Pas knew Alexie was going to join Stefan, the large furry dog jumped into the carriage and no one could pull or coax him out. A couple of burly men from the barn came to help, but Pas bared his sharp teeth at them.

The men finally gave up. Pas got into the seat beside Alexie, sitting like a passenger. When Alexie looked at the dog, he was sure Pas was smiling.

Now in Zagreb, at the door of Stefan's inherited building, Alexie and Pas patiently waited for someone to answer their knock. Alexie lifted the brass knocker again and pounded a bit more forcefully.

As soon as the door opened, Pas brushed past a very startled Ignatz, who was now dressed in new black pants and a white shirt. He wore a white apron tied at the waist making him resemble a waiter.

"I'm here to see Stefan Vladeslav." said Alexie, aware that the old man was not sure what to do or say.

Recognizing the voice, Stefan called, "Alexie!" He hurried to greet him. To Ignatz he said, "This is Gospodine Lucas, using the polite form for Mr.

Stefan pulled some krone from his pocket and gave them to Ignatz, "Go buy some vino and good cheese. Oh, and some chivapcici and onions. Don't forget bread."

Stefan shook Alexie's hand. "I am so happy you are here. I really need advice." Then again to Ignatz, who was heading for the door, "Find a nice cloth...when you return set the table."

Stefan asked excitedly, "How did you think to bring Pas? I am delighted you thought of it."

"I didn't." admitted Alexie, looking around the room which was a bit brighter now with cleaner windows and the shutters opened. "He got into the carriage and we couldn't get him out."

Seeing the gambling tables Alexie asked, "Are you planning on doing what Magda did?"

"Come in here," said Stefan, ignoring the question. "I have to show you this room."

Stefan stepped back and indicated that Alexie enter the door first. So stunned was Alexie, that he halted in the doorway with Stefan nearly bumping into him.

"Sveta Maria," said Alexie in a hushed voice. It was far more than he had expected from Anton's description.

"That's what I said when I saw this room." said Stefan. "Can you believe what is here?"

Alexie wandered about the room looking at the walls hung with paintings, while more were stacked in rows against one wall. Along another wall were rows of rolled hand loomed Persian carpets. Bronze statues, some as tall as a man, were on another side of the room. Heavily carved chairs with huge lion paw feet were among the treasures.

There were so many items and stacks that only a narrow path was available for access to the massive desk, the top covered with cloisonné vases and porcelain figurines.

Stefan waited excitedly for Alexie to say something. When he did speak Alexie asked in wonderment, "How did Magda ever acquire such treasures?"

"She didn't." said Stefan. "I found notes and a ledger in the desk. All of this belonged to the Turk."

Alexie, made his way through the narrow walking space looking at the accumulation. "My first thought is that Magda took these things in place of gambling debts." he said.

"Magda didn't, but I know the Turk did, because he took my mother's earrings in exchange for my debt."

Stefan's throat tightened when he said, "I found my mother's earrings in a drawer." He turned from Alexie not wanting the man to see the tears…tears reminding him that he brought so much grief to his family by his gambling and then running away.

"Aside from the value of the property," said Alexie, "I think you have a fortune here."

"What do I do with it?" asked Stefan. "I am not a shop keeper and I certainly don't know the value of these things."

Stroking his chin, Alexie said, "I think we need someone to come and look at the paintings. I am not sure that one person would know the value of everything." He ran his hand over one of the rolled Persian rugs. "Feel this rug." He said, admiring the softness. "We need to find experts."

"Do you know such experts?" asked Stefan.

"No," said Alexie studying a painting signed Boudin. "We have to do some searching.

"As soon as Ignatz comes back with our lunch and we've eaten, let's go for a walk. Perhaps we can find some help." said Stefan.

Yesterday, before Ignatz shopped for food or new clothes, he visited the lovely church Sveti Marko, with its beautiful white and red tiled roof. It was located nearby in the upper part of Zagreb. He lit a candle for Magda and said a prayer for her.

Today, before doing his shopping, Ignatz stopped to buy a bouquet of flowers to take to the spiritual kamenita vrata, the last remaining stone gate built in the 13th Century. In 1731 a fire in this area did not destroy the painting of the Virgin Mary and Christ Child, signifying this spot as a holy place. So for that reason, Ignatz made a quick trip to say a prayer for Magda, the only friend he ever had.

After a very nice lunch of the chivapcici sausages and a surprisingly good wine that Ignatz purchased, Alexie and Stefan, with Pas who would not stay behind, walked to the center of Zagreb.

"We need to buy a leash." complained Stefan, "This rope isn't very elegant."

"Well, he is a country dog." said Alexie with a laugh.

Stefan was surprised that he enjoyed walking through the square among all the peasants who were selling their food or handmade items. When he had been a student in Zagreb he had found the peasants with their bushels and wheel barrows full of things to sell, very boring. Now he found the market and people interesting. The smell of the penned goats and sheep, mingled with the fresh vegetables and flowers seemed to stir something in him. He was ashamed that he had not appreciated his roots.

The two men paused to watch a man deftly weave branches the diameter of a finger into a basket. The finished baskets he had for sale were large and sturdy.

"I think I'll send Ignatz to buy one of these." said Stefan, admiring how swiftly the old man's fingers moved in and out fashioning the basket.

Stefan's family had more education and money than the peasants but, this is who he may have been without the money.

A man walking nearby smelled of hay. Stefan imagined the man may have slept in an open wagon on the way to market, using hay as a bed.

Stefan especially noticed the smell of garlic. He did not remember being aware of the strong smell of garlic in France or Italy.

Alexie stopped at a table covered with assorted leather straps.

"Look," he said, "perhaps we can have a collar made for Pas."

The man behind the rough hewn table was as dark as the leather he was selling and his face was wrinkled from years of squinting in the sunlight. He was a small man with strong looking hands. The leather apron over black pants was the type worn by blacksmiths.

"Can you make a collar for this dog?" asked Stefan, pointing to Pas, who sat staring at the man.

With some reservation the man came from around the table to look at Pas. Tentatively he put his hand around Pas' neck to check the thickness.

"Dah, yes. I can make a collar. Are you going to use the rope, or will you also buy a leash?" he asked, wiping the sweat from his brow with the back of his hand.

In a matter of minutes he cut down a belt and punched new holes to adapt to Pas' neck. He then took a long strip of leather which had been meant for a whip and transformed it into a leash.

He happily took the money Stefan offered and kept the rope used as Pas' leash.

Alexie laughed looking at Pas. "I have never seen such a dog. Look at him," he said. "He is walking as if he is proud of his new collar."

CHAPTER 20

Back at Vladezemla, Katya was not yet over the shock of finding out that the girl she thought to be her sister, was not. She had loved the frail Anka and intensely disliked Anka's husband, Elia.

It had been the evil Elia who sold Katya to the Turk. She shuddered to think what would have happened if she had not escaped. It was Destiny that sent her Godfather, Milan, to find her hiding in the bushes and it was Milan who brought her here to Vladezemla.

She was sitting in the tall grass on the hillside overlooking the valley. *So this was where she belonged.* What would her life had been if she had spent her childhood here with Sofie? She remembered Stefan's mother, Ernesta. Katya was sure that greedy, bossy woman would have made her childhood unpleasant.

Destiny! Klara often spoke of destiny as if it were a power that formed lives and events. *For what reason had Destiny put Katya in Selna? Now Destiny had put Katya where she belonged. But, did she belong here? Why wasn't she happy here? It still didn't feel right.*

Below, in the distance she could see the Gypsy camp. She thought, *I need to talk with Valina.*

Queen Valina was special to Katya. Also, strange as it was, Valina and Lucia Kurecka, who is Katya's grandmother, were the best of friends. These two women were each so different, and yet as women, so much alike. Lucia was the daughter of a successful importer. She lived in a gorgeous house on a hilltop overlooking the Adriatic. She had married and loved one man her entire life.

Valina was a Gypsy. She was a Queen, a fortune teller, and once a beauty having had many admirers and lovers in her lifetime. She lived all her life in a rolling caravan, never belonging anywhere.

When Valina would travel through Trieste, she always stopped at the hilltop house of Lucia and the two women would sit on the stone terrace and talk for hours. They were kindred souls, sharing a bond neither Sofie nor Alexie could understand. Lucia's and Valina's friendship did not concern Katya, for she loved them both.

Somewhere in the distance, Katya heard a flute playing a soft sad melody. She stood up and looked over the hill and could see a man with a flock of sheep in the distance. The music probably came from him.

Katya turned back to sit on the grass. She had not heard Zolton come up behind her. She was startled when he touched her shoulder.

Pleased to see him, she laughed, "Where did you come from?"

He had been her very first friend when she escaped Selna. Handsome Zolton, a true Gypsy with dark shiny hair, almost black eyes and tanned skin, had met her in the woods, when she and her Kum Milan, stopped to rest. Milan had gone to a nearby farmhouse for food, while Katya wandered off. She had been fascinated to discover Zolton was a Gypsy. He was the first Gypsy she had ever met!

At that first meeting, Zolton took Katya to meet his grandmother, the Queen of the Gypsies. Valina was a true Gypsy and a mystic. She knew Katya would be in danger and gave her the bracelet Katya never removed from her wrist. It was the bracelet which saved her life when the Turk came to Vladezemla.

Katya seldom wore blue, but today her full skirt and long sleeved blouse were of blue cotton cloth. She sat on the grass and straightened out her skirt. Zolton was dressed in brown tight pants with a matching vest over a cream colored shirt, with full sleeves tight at the wrists. He seated himself next to Katya.

They were comfortable with one another. They were great friends.

"When are you and Roha going to marry?" she asked.

The Gypsy girl, Roha, was not pretty, but seductive in her manner. Wild curly dark brown hair framed her plain face. She always wore gold earrings and coin necklaces. And most of all, Roha disliked Katya intensely. She was jealous of Katya…jealous because Queen Valina was terribly fond of Katya and always visited the house where Katya lived whenever the caravan went through Trieste. Roha had no way of knowing that Valina visited Lucia and not only Katya.

"I don't know." said Zolton answering Katya's question while putting a cigarette to his lips. He struck a match on the sole of his boot and lit the cigarette.

"My mother does not want her as my bride, but Grandmother does." He blew some cigarette smoke into the air. "She made a promise long ago to watch over Roha. That was when Roha's father died." Zolton laughed softly, "I think Roha's father and my grandmother were more than friends."

"Don't you want to marry her?" asked Katya.

Zolton sighed deeply. He looked past Katya to the valley below where the caravans were camped. He could see some women preparing food in large pots over fires and others chasing after children.

He was quiet for a while and finally said, "I don't care. It doesn't matter. I can't have the one I want...so, I will make my grandmother happy and marry Roha."

Katya playfully slapped his arm. "Who are you in love with?" Then she added, "I have never seen you with anyone else or heard you speak of anyone."

Zolton stamped out his cigarette on a rock then flicked it out into the grass. He took another deep breath and let it out slowly. He turned and looked Katya full in the face, the face he had fallen in love with from the moment they met. He stared deep into her eyes, as if trying to reach her soul.

Neither spoke. Katya's eyes were glued to Zolton's. Her eyes grew wider as she realized what he meant. Her heart started beating faster, her eyes blinked. They were leaning towards one another...their faces getting closer and closer, until their lips met in a fierce kiss. They kept kissing falling to the grass. Feelings Katya had never experienced before now burned within her. She didn't want to let Zolton go. They pulled at one another in the heat of passion.

Ivan had come to the hill to sit with Katya. He felt that whatever they once had was gone but...perhaps, just maybe...it could ignite once again.

He saw Zolton and Katya in the grass. He was not angry...he was sickened by the sight. He limped away slowly, unseen.

Ivan wasn't the only one who saw Katya and Zolton. Roha had followed Zolton from the camp.

CHAPTER 21

Ignatz, in just a couple of days, had undergone a transformation. He was clean, dressed nicely, ate better than he had in a long time and had a proper position with the new Gazda. He even had gotten a haircut and a mustache trim. He looked younger and felt younger. He was no longer a vagrant hiding in an abandoned building telling himself he was a caretaker. He had a position! Ignatz wasn't sure who Stefan or Alexie were, but they were people of quality...that much he deduced. He was proud to be working for Stefan.

Alexie and Stefan were seated at one of the gaming tables, now used as the breakfast table. Their shirtsleeves were rolled up, but they were not sure what to do after eating. Ignatz poured the coffee into delicate Czechoslovakian cups found among the treasures in the office. He poured simultaneously hot milk from one pitcher and coffee from the other.

Taking a bite of the nut roll, Alexie said, "This is wonderful oranyache. Do I dare say it is even better than Klara's?"

"Where did you get this?" Stefan asked Ignatz.

"A woman in the square sells fresh bread also mak rola...poppy seed rolls." said Ignatz.

"Get the poppy seed roll for tomorrow." said Stefan.

Alexie sipped his delicious coffee. He dabbed his lips with a napkin and said, "I wish I could be here tomorrow to sample the poppy seed roll, but I must leave today. I worry about Sophie." Then he laughed, "Alas, sleeping in a room once used as a brothel, didn't give me any interesting dreams."

Slipping a piece of nut roll to Pas who waited patiently at his side, Stefan said, "I hate to see you go. It has been wonderful having you here to advise me."

"I haven't advised you." said Alexie.

"Yes, you have." said Stefan. "Just giving me your opinion and good company has been so helpful." Again he said, "I will hate to see you leave. I will miss you."

Seeing the imploring eyes of Pas, Alexie also passed him a piece of nut roll. Alexie said, "This is an exciting adventure for you, Stefan.

If Sophie didn't need me and I didn't need to get back to Trieste, I would love to stay and see what the future holds for you."

A loud knock at the door, startled the three men. Only Pas didn't look away, his eyes fixed on the remaining nut roll.

Ignatz hurried to answer the knock, while Stefan and Alexie looked toward the door.

Alexie said, "You don't suppose Anton has returned."

Framed in the open doorway was a stunning woman, a tall slender red haired young woman looking as if she could be a model for Charles Dana Gibson.

On her head was a large white picture hat sporting a black ostrich plume. Her high-necked blouse was white cotton the sleeves puffed at the shoulder and slim at her wrist. The skirt she wore was black satin, tight at the waist and flowing loosely to her high buttoned shiny black shoes.

Both Stefan and Alexie rose from their chairs. Ignatz hurried to Stefan, handing him the card the woman took from her metal chain purse.

It read: Barbra Pressler, Kunsthandler, Ilmenau, Deutchland.

Stefan stared at the beauty in the doorway as he handed the card to Alexie to translate. Alexie had learned some German while studying law.

"I think it means she is an art dealer." Alexie said, handing back the card to Stefan.

Stefan hurried to the door. "Please come in." he said, surprised by her arrival. How could such a lovely creature be in business? Women this beautiful were married or kept by wealthy men.

Barbra Pressler, art dealer, entered the room. This elegant woman glanced around, looking at the gaming tables. She said in Croatian, with a thick German accent, "Hmm, this could be a nice casino with a brothel upstairs."

Seeing the surprised looks on Stefan and Alexie's faces, she laughed a wonderfully warm laugh and said, "Is a joke. When I asked the concierge at the hotel how to find you, he told me what business had been here."

Alexie nudged Stefan's arm reminding him of his manners.

"I am Stefan Vladeslav and this is Alexie Lukas, my advokat."
He saw no reason to explain Alexie's connection to the family.

"Please sit and have some coffee. We have some very good nut
roll." Stefan looked for the nut roll, while Alexie held a chair for
Barbra.

Pas was two feet away finishing the last of the stolen nut roll.
Barbra noticed the dog and laughed, "Well, he must have thought it
was very good."

"Ignatz, go buy more pastries." ordered Stefan

"No, don't bother. I have had my breakfast, but I would like
some coffee." she said.

Alexie and Stefan both sat down observing the red hair under the
beautiful hat. The hair was not the deep rusty red like Katya's, but a
soft golden red. Again, like Katya, she had green eyes, but not as deep
and dark. Instead her eyes were light green and Stefan thought they
were almost luminescent. For that matter, he even thought her skin
glowed.

Sipping the coffee, she nodded and said to Ignatz, "Das ist auch
gut...this is good." Ignatz was honored that such a lady would
compliment him and his face broke into a great smile.

Alexie asked, "How did you hear about us?"

"It seems you are the talk of Zagreb." she said, as she pulled a
ten inch long hatpin from her hat, the end of which was adorned with
a large jet black jewel. Her red hair was loosely rolled on the top of
her head, in the fashion of the day.

Ignatz was by her side, taking her hat. He placed it and her metal
chain purse on a nearby table, first wiping the table top clean.

Alexie and Stefan exchanged confused looks.

"I don't understand." said Stefan. "What is being said? Who is
talking about us?"

Barbra took another sip of coffee. She could see they were
anxious for her to speak. She dabbed at her lips with a napkin. She
was toying with them, the way beautiful women do when they know
they are being admired.

"Well...let me see," she said slowly. "First I heard that a woman named Magda was back and was looking for girls to work upstairs." She waved her hand upward, indicated the rooms above. "Then, I heard that a mysterious man was living here. And...oh, yes, his servant has a lot of krone to spend."

Both Stefan and Alexie stared at her, not sure what to say.

She burst out laughing. "I make a joke again." She raised her cup to signal Ignatz for more coffee and he was immediately as her side.

"The truth is that I overheard a conversation while dining at the Palace Hotel." She sipped her freshly poured coffee and gave Ignatz another smile of approval.

Continuing, she said, "At the next table was an attractive woman, one I did not take to be a wife." Here she smiled knowingly, "Perhaps more of a companion? The woman mentioned that she knew Magda." She looked sideways at Alexie and Stefan, waiting for them to get her meaning. Satisfied they understood, she said, "The woman spoke of a room full of paintings and antiques. She also said the room was always locked, but that once, when she was in the gaming room, the door was opened slightly and she could see inside."

Barbra set down her coffee cup. "Time to get to work." she said with authority as she stood up. "Where is this roomful of artifacts?"

Stefan and Alexie stumbled to their feet. The authority this beautiful woman demonstrated bewildered them. Alexie expected Stefan to say something...anything.

But, Stefan didn't say a word. He led the way to the room of stored items. The door was not locked. He pushed it open and stepped away so Barbra could enter.

She paused, just as everyone before her who saw the room for the first time, had done.

"Ach...himmel. Oh, heaven!" she exclaimed.

Slowly, she walked through and touched various items almost reverently. Stefan and Alexie stood in the doorway, not wanting to crowd her as they watched her mentally assessing items.

After a few moments, Stefan asked, "What do you think, Miss Pressler?"

"Call me, Barbra." she said, "And, may I call you by your Christian names...Alexie and Stefan?"

Both men nodded. "Of course." said Stefan.

"Well, first...has anyone seen these things?" she asked.

"Only my father and Alexie and of course Ignatz." said Stefan.

"What do you know of Ignatz?" Her hands were on her hips, as she faced Alexie and Stefan.

"If you are wondering if he can be trusted, he has lived here as a caretaker for two years, I believe I can trust him."

She was only half listening. Her attention was diverted by a painting. "I believe this a Braque and that one a Leger." Barbra stood in the center of the room and thought aloud, "What can we do with this? Where will we go with it?"

Stefan said, "Whatever you suggest will be fine. We don't know what to do with any of this."

Alexie grabbed Stefan by the sleeve and pulled him out of the room. "What are you thinking?" he demanded. "More to the point...what part of your body are you thinking with?" Disgusted he added, "We don't know her! When did she become the Gazda here?"

"Of course, you are right." admitted Stefan. "But, look at her...isn't she fascinating?" Stefan watched as Barbra held a painting up to the light, examining it. A stream of sunlight played on her hair and it appeared to sparkle.

"Boze moy...my God! What am I to do with you?" said Alexie frustrated.

A troubled Alexie hated to leave Stefan alone with Barbra Pressler, but he needed to go for a walk, he needed to think. They knew nothing about her. Was she really an art seller? Could she be trusted? Was Stefan capable of thinking clearly because of his obvious fascination with her?

Alexie was now walking along the ulica with his eyes down, deep in thought. Sofie was his first priority and yet...he felt he should stay with Stefan. The way Stefan behaved around Barbra was as if he had never left Vladezemla. Whatever sophistication he had, seemed to disappear when she was near.

Alexie found himself on a familiar street. He looked up and recognized the building with the sign, J.Popovich, Ljechnik. This was the doctor he had recently taken Sophie to see.

Without a moment's hesitation, he opened the door and went in.

He nearly bumped into the handsome doctor, who was taller than Alexie.

"I was just going out for lunch." said the doctor. "Can this wait or do you need to see me now?"

"I am not ill, but I need to talk with you." said Alexie. "It is rather important to me."

The doctor put out his hand in greeting. "I remember you. You brought your wife to see me, not so long ago. Is she alright?" he asked, concerned.

"May we talk while you eat?" asked Alexie. "Let me pay you for your time."

Dr. Popovich remembered Sofie. He remembered that Alexie and Sofie had behaved as if this was to be her first child, while the doctor was aware that Sofie had at some time given birth.

Later, seated at an outdoor dining area, under a blue umbrella, the doctor and Alexie each had a cold glass of pivo…beer in front of them. Alexie refused food. He was in no mood to eat. The doctor had a huge smoked sausage with onions and sauerkraut.

"So," started the doctor, "How is your wife?"

"She is weak and has trouble keeping food down." said Alexie.

"Is that what you want to ask about? Are you asking if I have any medicine to help her feel better?" The doctor cut into his sausage with a knife.

"I need to know how serious this is…should I be with her?" Alexie looked away a bit embarrassed. "I believe I am needed here in Zagreb for awhile, but worry that I should be with Sofie."

Dr. Popovich was a strong, well-built man. His face handsome with clear skin. His eyes showed wisdom and compassion. The touch of gray at his temples only added to his good looks. He put his fork down and looked at Alexie, "There are some women who carry a baby and can work in the fields every day. Your Sofie is not one of these women. She will be sick until the day she gives birth. I have no medicine for this. Some women must just rest for they will feel ill the entire pregnancy. Once she has the baby, she should be fine." He picked up his fork again, "Is that how it was before?" he asked, looking directly at Alexie.

Alexie was surprised by the question. "You knew?" he asked, his eyes wide in surprise.

"I knew." he replied. Then, he continued, "I don't believe you need constantly to be at her side. Is she with family or friends? Are there people to care for her?"

Alexie nodded.

"Then, do what you need to do and don't worry. God watches over us all." He put a piece of sausage in his mouth and smiled at Alexie.

Alexie hurried to Jursiceva Street where the post office was located. In front of the two-story building was a vehicle larger than a touring car. The postal vehicle was enclosed with a covered rack on top for packages. It would take his letter to the post office in Petrinja, then from there, it would be taken to Vladezemla.

Alexie obtained some paper and an envelope at the post office. He wrote Sofie explaining that he had seen Dr. Popovich and felt confident that she would not be in any health danger.

He didn't go into any detail about the art seller, but wrote that he felt Stefan needed him for a few more days. Alexie included greetings to everyone and much love to his Sofie.

When Alexie returned to the gaming house, it now looked like a warehouse. Items had been brought out of the cramped office space and spread out on the various tables.

Barbra had a cloth tied around her waist for an apron. She was directing Stefan and Ignatz in the placing of items.

"Careful, careful!" she admonished. "You don't want to break that porcelain nude." Seeing Alexie, she said, "Good, you can help with the chairs.

Alexie removed his suit coat, folding it so that the lining was on the outside to keep the outer coat clean, before placing in on a chair. He stood still, not helping.

When Stefan came out of the office, carrying a large Chinese Urn, Alexie asked, "What terms have you agreed on? What will be Miss Pressler's commission?"

Stefan put the urn down. "We haven't discussed such matters."

Overhearing Alexie, Barbra said, "And we should. Come, let's sit. I need paper."

Ignatz came running with several sheets of paper from the desk along with a bottle of ink and a dip pen. He even thought to bring an ink blotter.

"Coming to Zagreb was meant to be a holiday. I have no contracts with me, but I can write out the conditions."

She wiped her hands on the towel at her waist and dipped the pen into the black ink bottle.

Stefan was a bit embarrassed. He knew nothing about business. He knew all the principles of card playing, the formalities and the protocol of gambling, but nothing about shop keeping.

He sat at a side table and watched as Barbra wrote. She dipped the pen into the ink bottle repeatedly as she wrote. Alexie remained standing, looking from Barbra to Stefan.

Damn it! Alexie had to admit she was beautiful and obviously very smart.

No one spoke while Barbra wrote. She put down the pen and used the ink blotter.

"Here," she offered the paper to Stefan. Instead, Alexie took the paper, which was written in the German language.

"While you two discuss the contract, I want to freshen up. It is getting late and I should return to the hotel."

Ignatz led Barbra to the back living quarters where he had water and clean towels for her to use. When she was finished she came out removed the towel from her waist and put on her hat.

"I will return tomorrow morning." she said. "We can discuss any changes in the terms then. But, now I must leave." Stefan stood and shook her hand, as did Alexie.

Stefan asked, "May I escort you back to the hotel."

"It is not necessary." She waved good-by and went out the door. A perplexed Stefan watched from the doorway as she joined an older man, waiting outside the gate. He was dressed in a fashionable brown suit with matching bowler hat. Barbra took his arm and the two walked away.

Later that evening, Alexie and Stefan took a leisurely walk around the city. In 1862, the Zagreb City Council decided to build a coal gas factory. A year later some three-hundred gas lamps illuminated the streets and squares. In the evening, the city was made more beautiful with the glow of these lamps.

"I have only been here two days and I think I like it very much." said Stefan, waiting while Pas lifted his leg at the base of a street lamp.

"Miss Pressler couldn't by any chance have made you like Zagreb more?" asked Alexie, lighting a cigarette.

"Oh, well..." Stefan didn't want to talk about Barbra Pressler, so he said, "Did you know there is going to be an Airport in the neighborhood of Crnomerec? It is being built now."

"What about Vladezemla?" asked Alexie.

"Compared to Zagreb, Vladezemla is 100 years behind the times." They started walking again, following Pas' lead. "Have you heard of the English writer Oscar Wilde?" asked Stefan.

Alexie shook his head, no.

"The Croatian National Theatre recently performed his play IH." Stefan was thinking out loud, "The world is here, Alexie. Just look at all the cafes and the people in them. The people look to be from everywhere in Europe and even America. There are newspapers here with stories about other countries."

They stood waiting while Pas did some serious sniffing.

"I think I could restore the upstairs of Magda's into the living quarters it once was." he said.

"You would live here? Permanently?" asked Alexie.

"Yes," he mused, "I never realized what an exciting place Zagreb is. I remember, while I was here at school, I didn't like it very much."

From a nearby hotel, the sounds of a Viennese waltz floated in the air. "Listen to that." said Stefan. "This is the place for me."

CHAPTER 22

A makeshift cot with pillows was placed near the edge of the kitchen garden close to the chapel. Amidst growing tomato plants, fragrant dill, onions and cabbage plants, lay Sofie dressed in a white nightgown, enjoying the warm sunlight and gentle breeze that rustled the trees sending the scent of flowers her way.

Her light brown hair was braided and wound around her head covered with a broad-brimmed hat. She didn't want her skin darkened by the sun. Tanned skin was for those who worked in the fields. Sofie would never admit that she was vain about her light complexion.

Alexie had not returned from Zagreb. She knew Alexie would never stay away if Stefan didn't need him. She felt more relaxed when he wasn't hovering over her. Now, knowing she did not have a grave illness made the discomfort of pregnancy tolerable for Sofie.

The shadow of a stork crossed her face as it flew to the nest on the chimney. Sofie smiled. A stork on the chimney meant good luck.

Sofie was content. She was even happy. Katya...wonderful Katya was her real daughter. Destiny had brought the girl back where she belonged...with her real family. Stefan was back...not dead, as they had feared. And...he was a changed young man. He seemed more thoughtful, less selfish. Things were going well, she thought.

She didn't care about the gossip. Sofie however was disappointed with the villagers. They loved her when she was there with gifts for their babies. She gave crosses and rosaries when the children made their first communions. Now that she no longer lived in Vladezemla to give gifts, she was no longer the beloved Sofie. She was now the mother of the witch.

A shadow fell across her face. She opened her eyes to see her brother Anton dressed in his riding clothes.

"I didn't mean to wake you." he said.

"I wasn't sleeping." she said. "You look wonderful in your riding clothes. Are you going somewhere?"

103

Anton wore slim fitting brown pants, a cream colored shirt and a short jacket, trimmed with black stitching. On his feet were gleaming leather boots. He was pleased to find his packed-away clothes still fit.

"Ivan was gone all afternoon yesterday and he didn't come up today. I think I will ride to Marko's and see if Ivan is alright."

Anton kissed Sofie on the cheek leaving her to rest in the warm morning sun.

Anton rode slowly into the village, nodding to people as he passed them. They in turn acknowledged him and waved or said hello. Most of all they were surprised to see him. He had once been a familiar figure in the valley, but for the past two years, caring for his wife, he had seldom left his home. No one dared ignore him or be openly rude to him. After all, he owned all of Vladezemla and most of people were in some manner in debt to him. Either they owed him rent or payments on the land they hoped to own. He was the one they borrowed money from when they needed it.

The villagers learned their lesson two years ago when they openly taunted Ivan and Marko, or said rude things about Vera when the word was out that Anton was Ivan's father. For a very long time, no one dared approach Anton for a favor or money, not when they had openly ridiculed his family. The villagers felt guilty and embarrassed at what they had said, but most of all they knew they had hurt themselves by being stupid and saying too much.

Anton rode past the Gypsy camp as he neared the house Ivan shared with Marko and Vera Balaban.

The Gypsy children running and playing waved to Anton. He wondered how long they would stay. In the past the Gypsies would have a festival of sorts a few nights before leaving. There would be dancing, a lot of food, fortune telling, and amulets sold to the villagers.

Anton smiled remembering how annoyed Father Lahdra had been seeing the villagers buying amulets...superstitious, magical things to bring luck or love.

His smile faded when he recalled that it was on such a night that the Turk had invaded his house and tried to kidnap Katya. It was on that horrible night that the Gypsies found Ivan battered on the hillside. Anton shook his head to rid himself of those memories. That was then. He had today and all of his tomorrows to look forward to. He was pleased for now a new baby was to be added to the family and his beloved Stefan was home.

He was sorry he couldn't share this new contentment with his deceased dear friend, Lahdra.

As he entered the fenced in yard of the Balaban property, he saw Vera, older and rounder, but still attractive, scattering feed to the chickens. Seeing Anton, she only waved her hand in the direction of the blacksmith shed, calling out, "He is in back with Marko." Vera didn't bother with a greeting. She surmised Anton had come to see Ivan. Ivan came home the day before greatly troubled, refusing to tell his family what bothered him.

Anton could see Ivan sitting on the ground, his back resting against a wall of piled field stones. Next to him sat his other father, Marko, the blacksmith, a strong man with arms big as logs. Marko wasn't a tall man, less than 6 feet tall. His body was stocky and strong from working at the forge. He wore a sleeveless undershirt over black wrinkled trousers. Over that was a leather apron.

Seeing Anton, Marko waved a greeting to him. "Come and sit with us." he said.

Anton squatted in front of Ivan, who looked at his Godfather. He thought of Anton as his godfather and not his father, for it was Marko who in his heart was his father.

"Are you not well?" asked Anton. "Why do you sit here?"

When Ivan did not answer, Marko said, "I have been asking him that since he came home yesterday. He won't say a word." Marko looked at Anton and asked, "Did something happen up at the house?"

"I don't think so." said Anton. He sat down on the other side of Ivan. The two fathers just looked at Ivan and then at one another. Marko shrugged his shoulders in an, *I don't know*, manner.

Anton pulled a pack of Turkish cigarettes from his pocket and offered one to Marko, who took it. Ivan shook his head, refusing the offered cigarette.

The two older men smoked in silence for awhile. There was the sound of clucking chickens and a cow mooed somewhere near.

Anton looked at Ivan, saying, "You look terrible. You are pale. Your eyes are red."

It was as if Ivan did not hear Anton.

"Do you need a doctor?" asked Anton.

Still no response from Ivan, so Anton said, "That's it! We are getting a doctor. If we have to tie you to a bed, we will. You can't go on this way." He paused then asked, with a sob in his voice, "Are you in pain? Ivan, listen to me. We are not going to let you sit here. Something is wrong and we need to know what it is. How else can we help you?"

Ivan closed his eyes and tilted his head back against the wall. He didn't want to look at his fathers. He bent his good knee and braced himself more firmly against the wall with his bad leg extended.

Again, Anton and Marko looked at one another waiting for Ivan to speak.

"Moi Drago sin," said Marko, "My dear son, please let us help."

At last, in a low voice, Ivan said, "I've lost her. I knew she was gone to me, yet I had a tiny hope."

"Who?" asked Anton.

"Who else!" demanded Marko, "Katya, he still loves Katya!"

Anton asked, "Did you and Katya quarrel?"

Ivan's eyes were still closed as he shook his head, no.

"Then tell us." demanded Anton.

Still, Ivan did not speak.

"I am going to look for Katya." said Anton, "She must tell us what this is all about."

Anton started to get up, but Ivan grabbed his wrist to keep him from leaving. "No." Ivan said in a low voice. "Don't go. I don't want to tell you, but I will, if you promise to leave Katya alone."

Marko and Anton looked at each other in agreement and then nodded to Ivan.

Ivan started to speak. He cleared his throat. "Yesterday I saw Katya go to the wooded hill area west of the house." He took a deep

breath and slowly exhaled. "I wanted to be with her...to talk to her."
He dropped his chin to his chest and shook his head from side to side.
"I saw her there." Ivan stopped speaking.

Marko and Anton waited for Ivan to continue. When he didn't,
Marko said, "Moi sin...my son, please go on. You saw her..."
Ivan raised his head, telling what he saw was torture for him.
"She wasn't alone."

Again Anton and Marko exchanged looks.
"I saw her with someone." he said.
"Who?" asked Marko. "Who was she with?"
"She was with Zolton." said Ivan.

Anton said, "Well, that isn't so unusual. They have been friends
ever since Katya came to Vladezemla. In fact, Sofie tells me that
Queen Valina visits them in Trieste."

Marko studied his son's face. He knew his son so well. There
was more to this story. Marko asked, "Why didn't you join them,
when you saw them?"

"A yoy...I couldn't! I couldn't say a word." He looked at both
his fathers and said, "I couldn't watch. I turned and walked away."

It took the two older men a moment to understand what Ivan
meant. Both men were heartsick for Ivan. He had never stopped
loving Katya. The hurt and shock of seeing her making love with
Zolton was about to destroy him.

Ivan's mother Vera was nearby listening. She said with disgust,
"Kurva...whore!"

While Anton was with Ivan and Marko, Katya was again on the
hill waiting for Zolton. She thought about yesterday and their love
making and remembering it thrilled her. She leaned back on her
elbows, eyes closed and smiling, as the sun warmed her face. She was
happy.

It didn't matter to Katya that this had to be kept a secret. Who
knew, maybe things would change so that she and Zolton could be
together? She wondered if she could be like the Gypsy women, living
in a caravan, cooking outdoors, even selling things in open air

markets. In her mind it was a romantic life full of travel and adventure. Perhaps she could learn to tell fortunes, she mused.

Katya waited a long time, far into the afternoon, but Zolton never came. Several times she stood on the hill and looked down at the Gypsy camp, hoping to see him coming.

Katya knew it was time to go home. Perhaps Zolton had to go somewhere. She would wait for him again tomorrow.

As she neared the house, she could see a horse drawn wooden wagon in the road. She recognized the driver as a Gypsy.

Katya entered the house through the kitchen door. To her surprise, when she entered the dining room, she saw Queen Valina seated at the table. In all the years that the Gypsies camped in Vladezemla, this was Valina's first visit to the house. Across from Valina sat Sofie and in his usual seat, sat Anton at the head of the table. There were no cups or glasses with refreshments that one usually shares with a guest.

With a rosary in her plump hand, leaning against the wall was the troubled housekeeper, family friend, Klara.

CHAPTER 23

There were no greetings or smiles.

Anton said, "Sit down, Katya."

Katya sat across from Anton, whose face was pale and his expression one of pain. This is not what he expected, nor wanted. He had promised Ivan that he would not talk to Katya about Zolton. But, it was now out of his hands.

Queen Valina wore her sleek black hair with strands of grey pulled back in a bun. Her dark eyes were troubled and her lips were tightly pressed. She wore a colorful satiny blouse and gathered skirt of red and blue designs.

Sofie's expression was one of bewilderment. In the deepest part of her heart she had hoped that Stefan or Ivan would marry Katya, for it was common for cousins to marry in that part of the world.

Katya was the first to speak. "What has happened?"

She was looking at Valina, fearing that some harm had come to Zolton. Perhaps he was hurt, she thought, and that was why he didn't come to the hill.

"Is Zolton alright? Has something happened to him?"

Sofie emitted a soft moan. To Sofie, the questions confirmed what Valina had told them. Zolton and Katya were lovers.

No tears fell from Valina's dark eyes, but there was a teary glistening.

"Zolton will not be coming to see you." said Valina, her voice soft and low.

Katya's eyes grew wide. Surely Zolton didn't say anything. She just *knew* he wouldn't.

Valina would have preferred to ignore whatever it was that Katya and Zolton felt for one another. She loved them both and more to the point; she had known the lovely feelings of passion with more than one lover in her youth.

Valina continued, "We plan to speak with your local priest, Father Mika to perform a wedding. It is time that Zolton and Roha marry." Valina saw the stunned look on Katya's face.

"They should have been married long ago." continued Valina. "Perhaps if they had been married this would not have happened." She paused and added, "Roha saw the two of you on the hill."

A tear rolled down Katya's reddened cheeks. "But…we love each other." she said.

"It is a love that cannot be." said Valina. "You live in different worlds. Zolton is Romani, you are not. Roha has been chosen as he wife and that is how it is."

Valina waited for Anton or Sofie to speak, when they remained silent, the Gypsy continued, "I love you Katya, almost as much as I love Zolton. If this could be…if it were possible or acceptable, I would be happy."

Katya looked from Anton to Sofie. She asked, "Do you have anything to say?"

Anton shook his head and looked away

Sofie said in a sad voice, "If only he weren't a tsigan…" She didn't know what more to say. She did not want to offend Valina.

No one spoke for several moments. Sofie and Anton avoided eye contact with Katya. Only Valina looked directly at Katya.

"I love you, Katya." She said again and rose from the table. She did not say good-by or shake hands with anyone. Queen Valina slowly walked to the front entrance of the house and let herself out.

Anton cleared his throat and said, "I think I will sit in the chapel for awhile." As he passed Katya's chair he paused, tenderly placing his hand on her shoulder, then continued out through the kitchen door.

Sofie, still in her chair, looked at Katya. "I don't know what to say. I suppose I should give you some advice, but I don't have any advice. You must know this can't be. It is wrong."

Katya said nothing, only stared at Sofie who was feeling uncomfortable. After several more moments, Sofie said, "I think I will go to my room."

Katya did not offer to help Sofie up the stairs. Instead she remained where she sat with her hands folded on the table.

Klara stood away from the wall. She realized that she had forgotten about her painful knees while listening to Valina.

She pulled a chair close to Katya. She wrapped her arms around the girl and hugged her. Katya let go the tears she had been holding back and sobbed. Also, old Klara sobbed. Klara never knew what it was to be made love to. Perhaps that is why she cried with Katya. Only once had Klara been kissed. That was when she was a young girl and Anton had come home a bit tipsy. He kissed Klara and when she had kissed him back, it was as if he realized he had over-stepped himself. He let her go, apologized and left the kitchen. Klara had never been kissed again.

CHAPTER 24

Katya had gone to her room.

Downstairs Klara sat alone at the table, with a cup of chai...chamomile tea before her, untouched and growing cool.

The house was silent, except for the ticking sound of the pendulum swinging back and forth on the old German wall clock. The usual outdoor sounds of clucking chickens, barking dogs and whinnying horses weren't heard by the troubled Klara.

How had this happened? She wondered. How could two days change their happiness from knowing Katya was Sofie's daughter and that Stefan was at last home, into a mood that now resembled a death?

Lost in her thoughts and in the stillness, Klara nearly jumped at the sound of the gentle knock at the front door.

"A yoy...now what?" Getting up from the chair and smoothing her skirt, she went to the door.

"Luba!" She said, surprised to see Ivan's young sister-in-law.

"I knocked at the kitchen door, but no one heard it." said Luba. She was married to Nikola, Ivan's brother. Her light brown hair was covered with a babushka. She had a pleasantly round face her brown eyes fringed with long pale eyelashes. Luba was a sweet girl and everyone who knew her loved her.

"Come in." Klara moved aside to let Luba enter. "Is something wrong?" She couldn't understand what had brought the girl to Vladezemla.

"Nothing is wrong." She fibbed, not wanting to tell about Ivan's strange behavior. "I came to help. The family and I talked it over and decided that it would be fine if I came each day for a few hours to help with the cooking and cleaning."

"Oh, Luba, how wonderful!" Klara was pleased. "Could you start the bread dough?" She headed for the kitchen with Luba following close behind. "I really need some towels washed. Do you think you could go down to the river later and wash a few? Not everything, just so I have some for the kitchen."

Katya upstairs in her attic room couldn't relax. For the first time the small bed with the carved headboard, the matching chair and the mirrored chifferobe made Katya feel claustrophobic. For a brief moment the memory of the Turk, standing outside her door on that night two years ago when he tried to kidnap her, flashed through her mind. She wanted to get out. Go somewhere...get some air.

As Katya passed Sofie's room, she heard "Katya, is that you?"

Ignoring Sofie, she turned and headed down the stairs. She didn't want to talk about Zolton. She didn't want to hear Sofie tell her again that it was *wrong.*

Klara was not in the dining room. When Katya heard voices coming from the kitchen, she paused...hearing a familiar voice.

Katya planned to slip out of the house to be alone, but Luba's voice drew her to the door. She pushed the door ajar. There was that dear girl who helped her throughout that night nursing Ivan when the Gypsies brought his battered body home that fateful night.

Standing in the doorway, Katya said, "Luba, oh, Luba how nice to see you."

The two young women rushed to one another. Luba with her flour covered hands outstretched, so as not to touch and soil Katya's dress. Katya hugged Luba and kissed her on each cheek.

Katya felt a special warmth for Luba. The girl had only been fourteen when she married Nikola, but on that night when together they nursed Ivan, Luba behaved with the skill and manners of a woman. Katya felt that Luba genuinely like her and that made Katya happy. Not for a moment had Katya felt that Luba thought of her as a witch and for that she was grateful.

"I see you are making bread, but why are you here?" Katya asked.

Luba went back to the table and resumed mixing the ingredients. She said, "I will be here every day for a little while to help Klara. Punica Vera...mother-in-law, Vera will take care of the baby."

"I heard you had a boy. When can I see him?" asked Katya.

Luba did not invite Katya to her home, instead she said, "I will bring him one day and you can see how much he already looks like his grandfather."

Klara moved about the kitchen, finding a bowl for the dough to rise in. She felt relaxed as she heard Katya and Luba talking. *This is good*, she thought. *Katya needs a young friend and Luba might just be the one to help her think and talk of things other than Zolton.*

Klara stepped out the back door, careful not to knock over the long wooden flat full of drying poppy seed pods. It was covered with material so that the birds would not help themselves to the seeds. In a few days, Klara would shake the seeds out of the pods and store them in a jar.

She saw Anton standing outside the chapel door. He was smoking a cigarette, a worried look on his face.

Approaching him, Klara said, "I have kitchen and household help."

Seeing his surprised look she said, "Luba Balaban is here. That sweet girl will come every day for a while."

"Did you send for her?" Anton asked.

"No, the family talked it over and Vera is taking care of baby Nikola so Luba can help me." Klara stooped to break off some chive spikes to take into the kitchen. "Luba and Katya are in the kitchen talking." She said, "I think Luba is good company for Katya."

"Poor, Katya." Anton sighed.

Klara looked at Anton. "You aren't angry that she and Zolton got together? That she let herself be involved with a tzigan?"

"Who am I to judge what others do." he said softly.

Just then the kitchen door opened and Katya led the way, her arms full of coarsely woven towels. Behind her came Luba with a few tablecloths. Along side the three steps stood a handmade straw basket. The girls dumped their laundry into it. They each grabbed a handle and headed for the stone gate leading to the river, where the village women did their washing.

"Klara called after them, "Maybe it is too late in the day to do the washing. The towels won't dry before dark."

"We can bring them back and spread them out in the garden." said Luba.

Anton was pleased to see the smiles on the girls' faces. He said, "I will tie up a rope and you can drape the towels."

Mocking Anton, Klara said, "Yes, now you put up a rope. You never put a rope up for me."

"Be quiet, old woman." He said with a smile, pleased to see the pain gone from Katya's face.

Luba and Katya laughed happy to be together. Luba talked about baby Nikola and the cute things he did and how proud Papa Nikola was of his son. The two chatted about this and that on their walk to the river. They passed a few men on the road who nodded, then quickly looked away.

At the river, there were several women on their knees pounding their wash on the smooth rocks. With their strong arm muscles, the women would wring the water out of the wet cloth. Clothing was strewn across the bushes, drying. Some would be left over night, but Luba and Katya would take theirs back to the house.

As Luba found a spot where they could start the wash, Katya noticed some Gypsy woman at the river looking her way. She wondered if she knew them and should wave to them. Katya realized that the village women stopped their washing and stared at her. Luba was busy pulling towels out of the basket and did not notice anything unusual.

Katya had an uneasy feeling. No one smiled. No one nodded a greeting. She felt the hostility. She looked away. Even when she was called a witch, she didn't recall these looks...these looks of hate.

Katya started to kneel down next to Luba, when the first rock struck her.

They left the basket of unwashed linens and stumbled up the hill to the house, hearing rocks thudding on the ground behind them.

It was Luba who was crying, while silent Katya was in shock. Klara watching Anton tie up a clothesline, screamed when she saw the two women stagger into the garden.

115

Anton turned...his face going pale. Katya was bleeding. Blood trickled from her hairline, while an angry red bump was forming on her forehead. Her right cheek was already swollen.

Anton dropped the rope and hammer. He ran to Katya, lifted her in his arms, while Luba hurried ahead to open the kitchen door. Anton went through the kitchen, kicking open the door leading into the dining room. He went directly to the sitting room to the overstuffed sofa and placed her gently there.

Luba, still crying, brought a bowl of water and towels from the kitchen. It was Anton who took them and gently wiped Katya's wounds.

"Mayko Boze..Mayko Boze...Mother of God," repeated a nearly faint Klara.

From the second floor, Sofie called, "What happened? Who screamed?" She clung to the banister as she tried to hurry down the steps. Hearing the commotion in the sitting room, she turned in that direction.

"Sveti Isus...Holy Jesus!" she cried when she saw Katya lying on the sofa. Seeing Katya's bruised and sore face, she cried out again, "Boze moy...My God."

She went to the back of the sofa, so as to be out of the way of Anton and Luba. A sobbing Klara stood beside her, grabbing for Sofie's hand.

"What happened?" Sofie asked again. "Who did this?"

Not looking up while helping Anton, Luba said, "We went to the river to wash some towels. We never got started. I think it was the Gypsy women who threw the rocks."

Before Sofie could ask why Luba was here, Klara explained, "Luba will be helping us each day."

Not responding to Klara, Sofie said, "You say it was the Gypsies?"

Sofie said softly to herself, "Oh, Katya...why Zolton?"

Katya heard Sofie. She pushed aside Anton's hand and sat up. Still not crying, but with anger building in her, Katya asked, "And...why not Zolton?"

She stood up…swayed for only a moment, then realized she was able to walk.

Luba said, "Katya, you should rest. You may faint."

When Katya headed for the door, everyone started to speak at once.

"Where are you going?" demanded Anton.

"Please sit down." begged Sofie.

Katya stopped and turned facing them all, her hands on her hips. "I am going to have a talk with Valina." Anton started to move towards her.

"No! Stop." ordered Katya, "Valina is going to hear what I have to say. I am not a child. Stop treating me like one!"

Katya, bruised and battered and very angry, started down the road to the Gypsy camp.

"Stop her." Sofie begged her brother.

Anton shook his head, remembering the arguments with Sofie in Trieste, when she was determined to stay with Vincent. He said softly, "That was you eighteen years ago."

Luba flew out the kitchen door and leapt over the stone wall and down the hill taking a rough but shorter way to her home. Something inside of her urged her to tell Ivan what has happened and what was about to happen.

The sun was fading and it was dusk when Katya walked into the Gypsy camp. She looked straight ahead, aware of the stunned whispers and even a few gasps. She expected a rock to be thrown, but there wasn't one.

Zolton's mother Kaja was adding wood to the cooking fire, upon seeing Katya she gasped. The slender dark woman hurried to Katya putting an arm around her shoulder. "What has happened? Come sit."

Katya did not sit. She went to the caravan steps and called to the open doorway, "Valina! Valina…come here! I want to speak with you."

No one could be seen. But many of the Gypsies were hiding out of sight, waiting to see and hear what would happen next, for no one dared speak in such a demanding manner to their Queen.

117

The look of annoyance on Valina's face quickly changed to one of shock when she saw Katya's face, which was starting to get blue in places. Valina hurried down the steps and ran to Katya, who pulled away when the old woman went to put her arms around her.

Katya stared at her once dear friend, the woman whose gift of the bracelet, with its ancient symbols, had saved her life.

"Take a good look, Valina." She said, "Look what your women have done to me."

Valina reached out a hand, wanting to touch Katya…to comfort her, but Katya brushed it aside.

"All this," she pointed to her battered face, "because, I fell in love with your grandson."

Tears were streaming down the face of Zolton's mother. She had never wanted Roha to be her daughter in law and this attack, she was sure was instigated by the jealous girl.

Katya and Zolton had only made love once, but by the way people were behaving it appeared they assumed this had been an ongoing affair. Something inside of Katya, some childish, revengeful impulse made her say, "And, if I have Zolton's child…you will never see it!"

Katya turned away from the two stunned women and cut across the camp towards the river, a shorter way back to the house than the road. No one stopped her, though she thought she heard Valina calling her to come back.

Dusk had turned to dark, but there was enough moonlight for Katya to see where she was going, or so she thought. This was the first time she had been off the road at night. She stumbled on some rocks, realizing these were not the rocks that made up the wall around Vladezemla.

She stopped walking. She thought she heard something… someone following her. She held her breath. She didn't move. There! She heard it again…the soft rustle of someone nearby in the grass. Katya was afraid to move from the rocks for fear of giving away her location.

Katya sensed someone behind her and turned. In the moonlight she saw the glistening metal of a knife. She instinctively threw up her arm and the blade bounced off her Gypsy bracelet, leaving a small cut on her arm.

Another figure appeared in the dark and grabbed the arm with the knife. There was the sound of a body landing on rocks.

"Let's get you home." Katya recognized Ivan's voice. He took her arm saying, "You have to help me, I've lost my cane. We can't take the time to look for it."

CHAPTER 25

It was early morning. As the cocks were crowing throughout the valley, Queen Valina once again was at the Vladeslav home. She didn't come in her caravan, but in the same open wagon as the day before.

The Gypsy driver helped her down from the wagon. Wearing a wool shawl against the morning chill, she went directly to the front door knocking loudly. She knew it was early, but it didn't matter. She needed to speak with Anton Vladeslav and it had to be now.

There were sounds of movement inside the house and finally Klara came to the door. Surprised to see Valina, she said, "Oh God, now what has happened?"

Valina pushed Klara aside and demanded, "I need to speak with Anton Vladeslav.

"Here I am," said Anton coming from the kitchen. "What is it now that brings you here so early?"

"We need to talk. Where is Katya?"

Valina walked directly to the dining table. She called in a loud voice, "Katya...Katya."

"No need to shout. I am here." said Katya, who also came from the kitchen.

Valina winced when she saw Katya. Her face looked worse than it had the night before. It appeared more swollen with bruises turning yellow and purple.

"I must sit down." said Valina, not waiting to be invited. Pulling out a chair at the table, she collapsed in it. She said to Katya, "You have to leave here." She said it with urgency in her voice. "I can't help you this time."

Seeing the confused looks on Katya and Anton's faces, Valina said, "You don't know that Roha is dead? She has been killed and we believe Ivan Balaban did it. His cane was found near her body."

"It was an accident," cried out Katya. "Ivan stopped her from stabbing me." Katya pulled up her sleeve and showed Valina the cut on her arm. "It must have been Roha who came at me with the knife

120

last night. She hit the bracelet instead." Again she showed her arm, noticing one of the stones had been knocked out of the bracelet from the strike. "Ivan pushed the attacker aside and we heard the fall. We didn't know it was Roha."

Valina put her hands to her face and turned her head from side to side.

"It doesn't matter how it happened." she said weakly. "It is done and one of our tribe is dead. There is no explaining it away."

Anton sat in the chair next to Valina. "You are telling us that there will be retribution? That no one will believe it was an accident?"

Valina took her hands away from her face. She sighed deeply. "There have been killings for love. It is not what we think is right, but we know that it has on occasion happened. Our people will think that Katya had Roha killed in order to have Zolton."

Sofie had been standing at the top of the stairs listening. She called out, "This can't be happening. My Katya isn't that kind of a person."

Valina rose from her chair. She rested her hands on the table and said, "I have come to tell you that I cannot save you if one of my people seeks revenge. Please listen to me and send Katya away. Send her to Lucia."

Klara standing in the kitchen doorway, her hand pressed over her mouth, for the first time in her life couldn't find anything to say.

"I must go." said Valina, taking Katya's hand and this time Katya did not pull away as she had the night before.

Valina turned Katya's hand palm up. She studied the lines in the small hand saying, "There is still danger in your path. I hope you will find where you belong."

Before she turned to leave, she said with a tremor in her voice, "God bless you all." Then she was gone.

Sofie made her way slowly down the stairs. "Anton, we must get Katya away from here." she said.

Anton was pacing, his hand to his chin, his mind racing furiously. There was no time to contact Alexie in Zagreb. Should he stay or leave with Katya? What about Ivan?

Sofie broke into his thoughts, "I am going with Katya to Trieste. Ivan should go with us, he is ours. He is family."

Anton, Katya and Sofie, all went into the kitchen where Ivan had spent the night in the tiny curtained space that had been Klara's sleeping area for many years.

Ivan was seated on a bench at the wooden kitchen table with a cup of herbal tea in his hand. "I heard," he said, "now what?"

Anton was thinking out loud, "I need to talk to Marko." He paused, remembering Vera, "Sveta Marija…Holy Mary, your mother! She will lose her mind when she knows you are leaving."

Over hearing the conversation, a worried old Klara came into the kitchen. To Anton, she said, "This means I will be here alone. Ivan can't handle the horses because of his weak leg…that means you must go along to drive the horses."

Another knock sounded, this time at the kitchen door.

In the doorway a very worried Marko and his other son, Nikola stood.

Nikola favored Marko in looks. He was husky and taller than Ivan, with dark brown hair. His brown eyes were sharp and clear.

Anton motioned for them to come in and sit. They sat one on each side of Ivan. The kitchen with its pots and pans hanging from the ceiling and the wall was becoming crowded with everyone in it. A stool was found for Sofie, while Anton, Katya and Klara stood.

Marko and Nikola, dressed in heavy woven work clothes, stared at Katya's face. "Oh, Katica," said Marko, "What have they done to you?"

She shook her head, waiving her hand in a dismissive motion. She didn't want to talk about her face.

Nikola said, "Luba will be here soon.

Klara said almost sarcastically, "I see Vera is not here."

Marko gave his cousin a look indicating, 'Don't start.'

Marko turned to his beloved step son Ivan, "What happened? People are saying you killed a Gypsy. Can this be true?"

Ivan, with Katya interrupting, told Marko what they had told Valina. Then they told of Valina's warning that they should leave.

Marko put his hands together as if in prayer and held them to his lips lost in thought. No one spoke waiting to hear what Marko would say.

At last he said, "When is Alexie expected to return?"

"We don't know." said Anton. "It could be today or not for a couple more days."

Marko said, "I could take them to Trieste, but it would be better if you did. We will look after Klara and Vladezemla."

To Marko, Ivan said, "Tata...they want to take me, also. I may be in danger."

With great sadness Marko said, "Of course, you are going." Then to Anton he said, "Destiny is taking Ivan away from the both of us."

There was more knocking at the kitchen door. A very angry Vera, with her daughter-in-law, Luba came into the already crowded kitchen.

Seeing the look Vera's face, Klara said, "Dragi Bog...Dear God."

Before Vera could say anything, Anton ushered everyone into the dining room. With side chairs pulled to the table, there was enough seating for everyone, while young Luba chose to stay in the kitchen to make coffee.

Vera, her head scarf a little crooked on her head, pointing a finger at Katya, said angrily, "You did this! We have had nothing but trouble ever since you came here."

Sitting next to Vera, Marko slapped the table with the palm of his hand. "Stop it Vera! This is not the time to vent your feelings. It is a time to decide what needs to be done. We have to do what is best for our children." He said "our" children including Katya who was after all part of the family.

Vera wouldn't stop, she said, "Now that everyone believes Katya is a Vladeslav we are to treat her differently...and we all know how she came to be a Vladeslav." The moment the words were out of her mouth, she regretted having said them.

Her beloved Ivan said softly, "And, Mamitza, we all know how I came to be a Vladeslav."

Embarrassed, Vera's eyes found Anton's. She quickly looked away feeling everyone's eyes on her. She was hurt, she was angry and she realized that she had lost her personal war against Katya. It was happening…Ivan would leave with Katya. It was something Vera had lied about and fought against, ever since that day two years ago, when she heard them talking the way lovers do; talking about leaving together.

Getting on with the problem at hand, Anton said, "Alexie's carriage is in the barn." Turning to Marko, he said, "Would you and Nikola hitch the horses while we get ready to leave?"

"I would help if I had a cane." offered Ivan.

Klara said, "Let me look around. I recall there is a nice walking stick somewhere." She left the room to search for it.

"Come Katya," said, Sofie, "Let's pack our things."

Anton, Vera and Ivan were left sitting alone at the table, the others gone to prepare for the journey.

Vera was across the table from her beloved Ivan, and sitting very near Anton at the head of the table. Anton reached out placing one hand on Ivan's and the other on Vera's hand. There were tears in his eyes. He took a moment to compose himself.

In a soft low voice he said, "I love you both. Forgive me if I have brought you pain." He closed his eyes, "Destiny brought us together and now she is pulling us apart."

Vera held onto Anton's hand tightly. Sobbing, she reached across the table taking Ivan's free hand in hers. She could no longer fight Ivan's destiny. If it were meant for him to leave her, then so be it.

Klara with a fine brass tipped walking stick in hand, stood away from the table, not wanting to intrude on such a private moment. She too had tears streaming down her round cheeks. She was no fortune teller, but she knew that life would never be same at Vladezemla.

CHAPTER 26

The trip to Trieste in the closed carriage had been a sad and stressful journey. An overnight stay at an inn where Sofie and Alexie had stopped before was a resting place for both the horses and the passengers on this trip.

It was an uncomfortable ride for Sofie, but she tried not to show it. The movement of the bouncing carriage made her more ill. It was much like the trip from Trieste to Vladezemla all those years ago, when a frightened Anton stopped at the convent for help.

There was little conversation during the trip. Ivan had killed a person...the Gypsy, Roha. It was an accident, but still, he was responsible for someone's death. He too, felt sick, but instead of a physical ailment, his was of the heart. Not only had he committed the sin of murder, but he couldn't get the picture of Katya and Zolton making love out of his thoughts. Hard as he tried, the memory kept returning.

Katya, very much like Stefan, blamed herself for the problems brought to the family. Stefan thought the death of his mother and problems the family endured were due to his gambling debt, while Katya believed her one afternoon of passion brought about the death of Roha and the upheaval of several lives.

Ivan rode on the outside seat with Anton who drove the carriage, while Sofie tried to rest lying on the seat inside the carriage. Katya sat opposite her mother, wishing she could do something to make Sofie more comfortable.

The two men, father and son, spoke little during the journey. Each was lost in his own thoughts, wishing they could see into future, wishing they could know what was ahead for them all.

Nearing the house in Trieste which was now her home, Katya could smell the sea. A tingle of excitement ran through her. She was home! She would see Lucia, whom she called Nona, and that was before she ever knew that Lucia was in reality her grandmother.

Mia, the young capable housekeeper and the wonderful Lucia, hearing the carriage traveling up the road to the hilltop house were excitedly waiting for its arrival.

Seeing Anton seated in the driver's seat instead of Alexie with Ivan, a stranger to her, disturbed Lucia. She sensed something was wrong.

When the carriage stopped, Lucia ran to the door and pulled it open. The sight of Sofie lying on the seat upset her, but when she saw Katya's bruised face, she screamed.

Katya jumped from the carriage, putting her arms around Lucia saying, "Please don't be upset. I am alright. It doesn't hurt." She lied.

Lucia pulled away from Katya, looking at the injuries. "What has happened to you? How did it happen? Are you alright?" The words tumbled from her lips.

Anton alighted from his carriage seat, helping Ivan down. He took the troubled woman's hand in his and said, "Madam Kurecka, we met long ago. I am Sofie's brother."

Fear clutched at Lucia's heart. The last time Anton was at this house was on the day Vincent died and she remembered Anton as rude, not allowing Sofie to stay for the funeral.

Lucia watched as Anton lifted Sofie in his arms from the carriage, carrying her towards the door, which the blond housekeeper Mia held open.

"Place her here." said Lucia, "Don't try to carry her upstairs." She motioned to the plush sofa in the main room.

The widow Lucia was dressed as always, all in black. Her only bit of color was the large carved coral cameo brooch at her throat, a gift from her beloved husband, Aleksy.

Ivan and Katya followed Anton into the house, while Mia helped the man servant bring in the hurriedly packed possessions.

Lucia with worry in her eyes asked, "Where is Alexie? Why isn't he here?" She was on the verge of tears. "My God, tell me what has happened!"

Anton turned from the sofa to the upset Lucia, saying, "Seniora Lucia, I apologize for distressing you by our arrival. Alexie is fine.

He is in Zagreb with my son. I promise to tell you everything. But, please may we have some water to wash with? We are very tired."

Katya took Lucia's hand and kissed it. "Nona, so much has happened since we went to Vladezemla." She introduced Ivan standing next to her, "This is Ivan, Sofie's nephew and Anton's son." Ivan bowed, but did not take Lucia's hand. Katya added, "He will be staying with us."

Lucia felt faint. Alexie was not here, Sofie was ill on the sofa and something terrible has happened to Katya.

Lucia sat in a chair near Sofie, who was still resting. Capable Mia showed Ivan and Anton to a room on the second floor, which was reached by a long wide stairway flanked by Nubian statues, like sentinels at the base of the staircase.

Katya said to Lucia, "I will be right back. I have been wearing this dress for two days, I want to change." And, she too went up the long stairway to her own room.

Now the top of the stairs, which Ivan had climbed slowly, he looked at the large room below. It was something out of the books Anton had given him to read, for he had never seen such a room.

Colorful Turkish rugs with intricate designs lay on the floor and large Flemish tapestries adorned the walls alongside large paintings. Curtains made of thick woolen weave hung beside the doorways ready to be pulled across the openings to bar any invading cold drafts. Marble statues befitting a museum seemed at home in this house, as did the many Asian vases and urns.

The plush sofa, where Sofie lay was in the center of two matching overstuffed chairs, one of which was occupied by a tearful, Lucia Kurecka.

In the room Ivan was to share with Anton was furniture he had never before seen. The furniture was not carved, instead adorned with patterns of various colors of inlaid highly varnished wood. Ivan did not know that this type of wood working was famous in Italy.

The bed was high and one needed a step stool to get into it. On the bed appeared to be a mound of feather ticked coverlets all white trimmed with lace edging. The fabric appeared more delicate and lighter in weight than the woven material he was used to at home.

Wearing a black skirt, black stockings, white blouse and a white bib apron, efficient Mia carried a large wash bowl, pitcher of water, and soft towels, placing them on a marble topped bureau.

Tired, Ivan sat in a side chair, stretching his leg. "I believe I will sit here for awhile." he said, watching Anton begin to freshen up. In a matter of moments, Ivan dozed off.

Downstairs, Anton found a tearful Lucia, sitting near Sofie, who was asleep. Seeing Anton, Lucia rose and took Anton's hand. She said, "You promised to tell me what has happened. Is Sofie as ill as Vincent was? I couldn't stand to lose her, too." The old woman began to cry, holding a lace handkerchief to her eyes.

Anton asked, "Where can we go to be alone?"

Lucia led Anton to her favorite place, the lovely terrace overlooking part of the Jadran, the Adriatic, this part known as the Gulf of Trieste. Her terrace garden was splendid with blooming roses and magnolias filling the air with their sweet scents. Near the entrance was a large rectangular cage, almost as tall as a man. It was on wheels and covered in wire mesh. It was a mobile aviary housing a variety of colorful song birds. Stone planters were placed near the entrance to the house and some along the terrace wall, all with colorful flowers.

Anton was immediately drawn to the wall, going there he looked over at the blue sea splashing against the shore far below and listened to the gulls overhead as they seemed to sail in circles.

When he turned away from the wall, he saw Lucia already seated at a table covered with an apricot colored cloth. A glass pitcher and some lovely glasses from Murano were placed on it.

Mia, who seemed to appear and disappear caring for the household, was pouring juice into the glasses. Anton had no idea what the pale yellow liquid was.

Seeing his look of wonder and surprise, Lucia explained, "That is the juice of pineapples. The fruit is brought to us from Africa on our ship."

An anxious Lucia said, her voice quivering, "It is time for you to tell me what has been happening. I cannot wait any longer."

Anton put his glass on the table. He folded his hands in his lap.
He sighed, "Let me start with the very best news first." He waited for
a reaction from Lucia, but there was none .Her dark eyes were fixed
on him.

"There is no need to be fearful for Sofie. She is only resting
because she could not sleep in the carriage." He saw Lucia glance
towards the house at the mention of Sofie. He went on, "You
see…Sofie is going to have a baby."

Lucia's hands covered her mouth in disbelief. She said in a
whisper, "Can this be true? At her age?" She dropped her hands into
her lap. "Did she see a doctor?"

"Yes, she saw a fine doctor who confirmed that she is about
three months pregnant."

Lucia jumped from her chair practically running into the house,
with Anton fast behind her. She flew through the doorway and
stopped at the sofa where Sofie was still sleeping. The woman gently
touched Sofie's smooth cheek.

She said in a very soft voice, "It won't be my grandchild, but I
will love it as if it were."

Katya, now changed into a simple dress of light green, was at the
foot of the staircase. She heard Lucia and went to her, taking the
woman's hand. "Come, Nona," she said, leading Lucia to the
outdoors again. "Let's go to the terrace."

Turning to Anton, she asked, "How much have you told her?"

"Only that Sofie is pregnant." he said, taking Lucia's other hand
as they went back to the table outdoors.

Lucia looked at them suspiciously. It was painful for the woman
to look at Katya's face, which was healing and looking better, but it
was still a disturbing sight.

Anton and Lucia were seated across from one another in metal
chairs padded with cushions. Katya kneeled beside Lucia. She held
both of Lucia's hands as she looked into the face of the woman she
loved dearly.

"Nona…" she began, "the priest in Vladezemla was Anton's best friend. He died a month ago, leaving his personal diaries for Anton to read."

Lucia started to speak, but Katya held up her hand, stopping her. She went on, "You see, Father Lahdra heard the last confession of the Mother Superior of the convent where Anton took Sofie when they left here and she was so ill."

Lucia was becoming impatient, what did this priest's diaries have to do with them and what did she care about a dying nun's last confession!

"Nona…" Katya could see Lucia's impatience, "Teta Sofie… I mean…you see, she wasn't sick, she was pregnant."

Lucia's dark eyes grew large in disbelief. Katya hurried on with her story, "The nuns thought the baby…that…I was born dead."

"What are you saying? Why are you saying these unbelievable things to me?" Lucia stood up, "I already love you as my own. Everything I have is yours and Sofie's. You don't have to make up such stories."

"But, Nona…it is true!" Katya was nearly in tears.

Anton went to Lucia. He took her hand in his and said, "Please let me talk." The two of them went to the terrace wall and sat on a stone bench, leaving Katya alone at the table. She couldn't hear him, but watched as Anton spoke to Lucia. He was explaining in detail about the ledger, about the confessions of the two nuns and how it was that Katya was taken to Selna. Katya could see the range of emotions on Lucia's face, first disbelief and finally acceptance.

With tears streaming down her face, Lucia with open arms, walked toward Katya. Katya rose from the chair as the old woman wrapped her arms around her.

"Mia Piccolina." Lucia kept repeating. "My little one."

Awake from his brief nap, Ivan watched the scene below from the balcony off of the room Anton and he were to share. He couldn't hear the conversation, but had an idea what was taking place.

He looked away from the terrace, far off into the distance where he saw fishing boats. Ivan was sensing an excitement within him.

Before him was a new world, one of adventure and opportunity. He could read, do bookkeeping and possibly more if he thought about it.

Ivan dragged a chair from the room onto the balcony. He placed it close to the rail. Sitting in the chair, his elbows resting on the metal rail, he stared out into the world and his future.

Anton left Katya and Lucia alone on the terrace. The two women, one so young and the other so mature, sharing the wonders of the mean trick Destiny played on them by separating them for so many years.

Sofie was awake when Anton came to sit with her. She asked, "How long have I been sleeping?"

He smiled at her, realizing just how much he loved his sister, "Long enough for me to tell Lucia that you are pregnant and that Katya is her granddaughter."

"Where are they?" she asked, trying to sit up.

"On the terrace," he said, and added, "By the way, what a beautiful terrace, the view took my breath away."

"I should go out there," said Sofie, "But, I am really too tired to leave this sofa."

As if summoned, Mia appeared with a cup of tea and a biscuit, setting them down on a tiny brass inlaid table from India. For Anton, she had a glass of vino.

Looking around, Sofie asked, "Where is Ivan?"

"I left him asleep upstairs in a chair. He was as exhausted as you."

Out on the terrace, Katya told her grandmother about her feelings for Zolton, about their one afternoon together and all the rest. She confessed to Lucia that she felt responsible for the death of Roha and for Ivan being exiled to Trieste.

There was a part of Katya's story that disturbed Lucia. There was the possibility that Lucia and Valina may no longer be friends. She was tremendously fond of the colorful Gypsy and especially of the woman's honesty. Lucia so enjoyed the time spent with Valina on this terrace talking of so many things.

Being the devout Catholic woman that Lucia was, saying her rosary daily, it surprised her that Katya making love to Zolton didn't bother her. Perhaps it was her age, for as one got older, one wasn't so quick to judge.

The five of them had a pleasant late afternoon meal on the terrace. Mia served Italian bread with olive oil for dipping, olives and cheese as an appetizer with the main meal being sardoni, fried sardines and squid. Anton and Ivan were both pleased and surprised that they enjoyed the meal, when they discovered they had been eating squid. Plenty of wine was on the table and the desert was a special Italian treat of canoli, the fried dough rolls filled with a sweet cheese mixture.

After the meal, Anton carried a very tired Sofie, who ate very little, to her room. Mia and Katya followed to help ready her for bed. It was early evening but she was exhausted.

Anton returned to join Ivan and Lucia on the terrace to enjoy the soft breezes of the late afternoon, sipping dark espresso from small delicate cups. The strong coffee was new to Ivan, who only knew the milk and coffee mixtures he drank at home.

The two men enjoyed the view, Lucia's company and smoking their cigarettes. Ivan and Anton were comfortable with Lucia. She had a way of making people feel at home with her.

Anton said, "I should be leaving for Zagreb."

"So soon," said Lucia. "I thought you might stay a few days."

"I thought I would leave tonight, but Mia tells me there are no trains from Trieste into Zagreb. That means I may need to hire a driver."

Lucia thought a moment and said, "Wait until morning. I can have a driver for you. You can take Alexie's carriage again and the driver can bring it back." She added, "You shouldn't leave tonight. The horses need to rest as much as you do."

Their conversation was interrupted by a man's voice. "Is Alexie back?"

Ruda Klarich, Alexie's right hand man at the law firm in Zagreb and now at Renaldi's Import Company, came out onto the terrace.

Seeing Lucia's guests and not knowing them, Ruda apologized, "Lucia, I am sorry for intruding. I thought Alexie was here when I saw the horses in the barn."

"Come sit with us." said Lucia, "This is Anton Vladeslav, Sofie's brother and his son, Ivan."

Both men rose and shook Ruda's hand. Ruda was a small, slender man, only 5 feet 6 inches tall. His eyes were hazel, his hair brown, parted down the center. His face was smooth, so that with his short stature, nice eyes and wavy hair, he would have made a pretty girl. There was nothing feminine about Ruda. Because he was small, he felt he had to prove he was tough. And he was tough, in a pugilistic way.

It had been Ruda who had gone with the local priest to Selna with papers drawn up by Alexie, when Katya deeded her property to her Godfather Milan.

Ruda reached for a clean glass and helped himself to some vino. He was used to coming to the house each evening to report the day's activities at the import company.

He asked, "When is Alexie coming back? I didn't think he would be gone this long."

"I will be leaving in the morning," said Anton. "Alexie can come back in the carriage. It may be another four days before he returns.

Ruda said, "We need him and Sofie. I can't take care of the accounts and the shipments alone. I am doing it, but I am getting behind in the bookwork."

Lucia made a suggestion, "Ivan will be staying with us. Perhaps he can help you?" She turned to Ivan, "How are you with figures?"

Anton answered for his son, "He has been keeping accounts for me at Vladezemla for the last two years."

"I could use the help." said Ruda, finishing his wine and getting up to leave. "I'll see you in the morning." he said to Ivan, shaking his hand and then Anton's who said, "Let me walk you to the door."

Ruda kissed Lucia's hand and touched his forehead in a salute to Ivan.

CHAPTER 27

Alone in the bouncing carriage on his way to Zagreb, Anton tried to curl up in the seat and sleep. His thoughts wouldn't let him drift off. Had Vincent lived and Sofie married him…well, that never would have happened, for Sofie's father would not have allowed it. But, if…if…Sofie had her baby in Trieste and lived with Lucia, the girl's life would have been so very different. If…Katya had been raised in that beautiful house and not taken to Selna, she would not have been sold to the Turk. If…Katya had been in Trieste instead of Vladezemla, she would not have been involved with Zolton and Ivan would not have accidentally killed Roha.

So many ifs…if…if…if.

Anton was glad to see the streets of Zagreb ahead. He was tired from jostling in the carriage, first traveling to Trieste and now to Zagreb. The smell of the land was different from Trieste. Here one could smell the earth, the animals and the vegetation.

He directed the driver to Stefan's new place and had him lead the horses to the back of the building. "Wait here," he instructed the driver, "someone will come to help you."

Anton knocked on the back door, the one that Ignatz used. When there was no answer, Anton turned the handle and finding the door unlocked, entered. It pleased him to see that Ignatz kept his living area so tidy and clean.

Anton went through an open door leading to the main room. His mouth fell open when he saw the transformation.

He saw a room full of cloth draped tables with a seating area for clients.

Alexie and Stefan were at a far table, towards the back of the room going over some papers. They hadn't seen Anton enter. It was when Pas the dog, stood up noticing Anton, that Stefan looked up. Seeing his father, he cried out happily, "Tata, Tata, how wonderful to see you." He hurried towards his father wrapping his arms around him. "What a wonderful surprise."

134

Alexie rose and joined them, shaking Anton's hand. Concerned he asked, "Is Sofie alright? Did something happen?"

"Sofie is fine. I will tell you everything shortly. First, could you send Ignatz to help the driver with the carriage and the horses?"

Seeing the confused looks on both Stefan and Alexie, Anton said, "The horses need to be boarded for the night, also the driver will be spending the night."

Stefan lifted a small brass bell from the table and shook it. The ringing sound brought Ignatz hurrying from the office near the front entrance, where Barbra had him working.

Ignatz smiled and bowed when he saw Anton. The transformation of the old unkempt caretaker to a proper looking competent man servant was a pleasant surprise to Anton.

Stefan said to Ignatz, "Help with the horses in back and see to the carriage. We will have a man staying with us tonight."

Alexie still felt there was a more important purpose for Anton's visit, something other than just stopping in to see how things were going. Alexie took a bottle of wine from a side table and some glasses. He moved the papers he and Stefan were going over, and set down the bottle and the glasses.

"Come, Anton. Tell us the news." he said.

Never in his wildest imagination could he have guessed what his brother-in-law had to tell them.

"Yes,Ta. Tell us what is happening in Vladezemla." said a happy Stefan.

Anton removed his coat and tossed it on an empty chair. He sat at the table with Anton and Alexie, aware that Pas was staring at him as if also waiting to hear the news.

He said, "Will we be overheard? What I have to say is private family business."

Stefan's mood changed in an instant, as did Alexie's.

Stefan said, "There is a woman working in the office, but she can't hear us. And if a customer comes in to buy something, she takes care of them."

Anton reached for the wine bottle. He filled his own glass, then the other two. In one swallow he emptied his glass.

He began, "Alexie, tomorrow you leave for Trieste." Before the surprised Alexie could ask a question, Anton re-assured him, "Sofie is fine, nothing to worry about. She is fine. We just…had to leave Vladezemla."

Stefan reached across the table taking his father's hand, "Ta, what is it?"

Anton began first with Ivan seeing Katya and Zolton making love. This surprised both men. The surprise became shock when they heard of the rock attack on Katya by the Gypsy women. There was dumfounded silence when he got to the part about Ivan accidentally killing the Gypsy girl, Roha.

By the time Anton finished the story and explained Valina's visit urging them to leave, for Katya's and Ivan's safety, the bottle of wine was empty.

Alexie felt ill. He felt he should have been with Sofie, instead of having a good time witnessing Stefan's new life adventure.

He said, "Perhaps, I should leave for Trieste now."

Anton said, "I know you are concerned about Sofie, but she is fine with Lucia, who, by the way, I find to be an interesting woman."

He added, "Also, the horses have been traveling for three days. Let them rest. Tomorrow is soon enough to leave."

"Poor Ivan." said Stefan. "What will happen to him so far away from home?"

Alexie said, "We can take care of him. I will find work for him at the import company."

"Ruda has already asked Ivan to be the bookkeeper for the time being." said Anton.

"I was thinking of Ivan's feeling for Katya," said Stefan. "How all this must have hurt him. Anyone could see how Ivan felt about Katya every time he looked at her." Stefan was silent for a bit, then added, "It will be hard for him to be near her, caring for her the way does."

Not wanting to discuss such a painful subject, Anton said, "I need to eat something. This wine on an empty stomach isn't good for me." He looked around for Ignatz, who as though he could read their minds, appeared with a platter of cheese and some pumpernickel bread.

The three men each took some cheese and bread. Anton asked between bites, "What were you studying when I interrupted you?"

Alexie said, "We were going over the accounts for the last two days."

"Yes," said Stefan, "We started out planning to only sell what we have, but people have been coming in to trade items as well as to sell. It appears what is known as our 'inventory' is growing."

Anton put down his bread and stared at them. "What do you know about trading or selling?"

"We don't." said Alexie and Stefan, almost simultaneously.

Stefan nodded to Alexie, indicating he should speak. "You see, Anton," Alexie said, "We only go over the figures...the accounting. It is Barbra who does all the selling and trading."

"Barbra?" Anton looked puzzled.

"She just appeared one day," said Alexie. "The next thing we knew, we had an art expert and a store manager."

Here Stefan interrupted, "Now, Alexie, admit that you weren't sure about her in the beginning." Then to his father, Stefan said, "She is amazing. She has sold some of the gambling tables...and," here he laughed out loud, "She has even sold one of the beds from upstairs as a historical item from Zagreb...of course, meaning Magda's brothel."

Alexie said seriously, "I don't know what Stefan will do when she leaves. This is her fourth day, but we know she will be leaving."

"Leaving?" asked Anton, "Why would she leave."

"Because she is only here on holiday, she lives in Germany." said, Stefan, looking across the room watching as a man and woman entered the front door. By their dress, they appeared to be Americans.

Barbra came out the office almost instantly, greeting the visitors. She wore a cream colored high necked blouse trimmed with lace at her throat and the cuffs of her sleeves. At her neck was a large oval brooch of golden amber. Her skirt was floor length, black in color, nipped at the waist flowing to her ankles. As always, her red hair was up in the Gibson Girl fashion.

"My God!" said Anton, in awe. "She is beautiful."

Reaching for a cigarette, Alexie smiled saying non-chalantly, "Stefan thinks the same."

Stefan's cheeks grew pink.

To change the subject and to take the attention away from himself, Stefan asked, "Did you see the sign out front?"

"No," said Anton, "I didn't notice any sign."

Alexie laughed again, saying, "You didn't see the huge sign? The sign reading: VLADESLAV KOLECIJA...Vladeslav Collection."

Anton's jaw dropped.

Stefan was watching Barbra, which he always did when she was with buyers. He saw her give a graceful wave in his direction. He rose, took the suit jacket from the back of his chair and put it on. He smoothed his hair and without a word to his father or Alexie, went towards Barbra and the Americans.

"Where is he going?" asked Anton.

Alexie smiled, for he found Stefan's new position as an art collector and connoisseur amusing. "He is going to meet the buyers, talk briefly about the Vladeslav collection, thank the people for coming and then bow explaining that he will leave them in the capable hands of Barbra."

Anton shook his head in wonder. He asked, "Do you suppose they will buy anything?"

"I'm sure they will." said Alexie, tearing a piece of bread in half before putting it in his mouth. "The wealthy Americans buy more than any others. It seems they can't get enough of European art or antiques." Without getting up, he reached for another bottle of wine at the table close by.

"Barbra makes arrangements for the packing of the items and has them delivered to the hotel where the travelers are staying." He added, "I must admit, she is an amazing business woman."

"And beautiful." said Anton.

"And beautiful." agreed Alexie.

They watched Stefan as he spoke with the buyers. He bowed, shook the man's hand then kissed the woman's hand before returning to the table. On his way, he looked every bit the connoisseur as he adjusted the angle of a vase on one table and then repositioned a figurine at another table. He paused giving the effect of deciding if it were presented at its best.

Anton stared in wonder at his son, while Alexie just chuckled softly at the acting done by Stefan.

When Stefan was again seated in his chair, with his jacket off, Anton said, "You looked as though you knew what you were doing."

"I am learning." was Stefan's reply.

Now, being serious, Alexie said, "How will you carry this off once Barbra is gone? You know that she is making you look very knowledgeable."

Before Stefan could reply, his father said, "Marry her, Son."

CHAPTER 28

Alexie, always easily bored just sitting, went out back to see the carriage and the horses. He also wanted to speak with the driver for news of Trieste. The driver was in Alexie's employ and when in Trieste, lived in a barn near the import company.

In what was now an art gallery / antique establishment, instead of a gambling casino, Anton looked around impressed. He sat alone at the table, far in the back of the room, near the stairs leading upstairs. After having seen the Nubian statues at the base of the staircase in Lucia Kurecka's Trieste home, he couldn't help but think a similar touch would be beautiful here.

Stefan was at the front of the room with Barbra and more buyers.

Curiosity drew Anton's attention to the stairs. He went up to what had been the living quarters of this wonderful old stone and marble house, before Magda bought it and it became a business.

Once at the top of the stairs, Anton followed the balcony encircling the second landing, giving an overall view of the floor below. Anton could only imagine the balls and gatherings that must have taken place in this grand house.

The first door he opened was to a large room, which may have been the master bedroom or even the library or sitting room. Each of the five rooms he looked into had tall glass windows, which opened outward. Instead of a fireplace, there was a beautiful ceramic heating stove with a ceramic chimney going to the ceiling in every room. As Anton wandered about, he was aware that all but the one large room had been made into bedrooms by Magda. He envisioned the rooms changed into comfortable and beautiful living quarters.

Back on the narrow balcony, looking below at the main floor, he thought a wall may have been removed from the section, where he had been sitting with Alexie and Stefan.

He slowly descended the stairs, marveling that he could be falling in love with this building.

Anton went outdoors as he had entered, through Ignatz's living quarters. He looked about the back yard. He saw Alexie talking with the driver in front of a building which Anton surmised was the barn or shed where the carriage and horses were being kept. There was plenty of room back here, where one could sit and dine...if one lived here. He walked along the side of the house on the road leading to the front. It was nice and wide with plenty of room for carriages to come and go. There was a short ornate iron fence surrounding the front of the building. The front needed tending, he thought. Flowers needed to be planted in the pots.

What he saw to the right of the doorway, affixed to the wall, pleased him more than he could have imagined. There was the large white sign with gold lettering, each letter outlined in black: VLADESLAV KOLEKCIJA.

Anton stared for some time at the sign, realizing he felt emotional seeing his name affixed to the building. His son owned this beautiful building. His son had a respectable business with people from everywhere coming to buy. Never had he thought the young lazy, shiftless Stefan would make him proud. But that was what he felt...great pride!

Back inside, again sitting alone at what he thought of as 'the family table', Anton looked to the front where Stefan and Barbra were with an elegantly dressed man. He watched as Stefan held up a painting and Barbra appeared to be pointing out the merits of the work.

Anton felt as though he was in a different world. It seemed almost unreal to him. As a youth at school here in Zagreb, he had loved the city, found it exciting. He recalled how happy he had been as a student. He enjoyed the debates with his classmates over current issues of the time. All these pleasant memories were stirring within him. He especially loved the Tamburitza music played at the outdoor kafanas in the evenings. Anton would have burst with pride had he known that in the year 1900, the tamburitza orchestra "Zivili Hrvatska" performed at the White House for President Theodore Roosevelt

Ignatz brought a bottle of slivovica and clean glasses and placed them on the table. "Hvala." said Anton, giving Ignatz an appreciative nod.

Anton poured himself a drink and sipped the plum brandy slowly, savoring the flavor. He put his glass down and with his elbows on the table, folded his hands together and supported his chin on them. He was thinking...and he was surprised by the lack of thoughts about his home. When he was at Vladezemla he constantly worried about the running of the place. There were constant thoughts of what needed to be done, who should do it and especially what the peasants were saying about him and his family. The realization that he didn't care about Vladezemla was a revelation to him. *How could he not care or worry about the land? The Vladeslav land.* Instead his thoughts were filled with ideas to renovate this beautiful old building.

A feeling of guilt passed over him. He took another sip of slivovica. *He couldn't remember when he last thought of Lahdra!*

He was so deep in thought that he didn't see Stefan and Barbra standing in front of him. When he noticed them, he quickly stood.

"Ta," said Stefan, "may I introduce Barbra Pressler?" And to Barbra he said, "This is my father, Anton Vladeslav."

Barbra gave Anton one of her dazzling smiles and said, "So, I meet the Papa. It is such a pleasure." She extended her hand. Anton found her accent charming.

Stefan had never seen his father kiss a woman's hand before. In fact, he had never thought of his father as sophisticated. He only knew his father at home as the land owner.

Anton pulled out a chair, offering it to Barbra. "No thank you." she said, "It is time for me to leave."

Ignatz appeared with a large cream colored hat trimmed with lace similar to the lace on her blouse. She smiled at Ignatz and placed the hat on her head. She took the gloves and purse Ignatz was holding for her. "I must go now." She made a small bow. "Tomorrow, I shall return."

Stefan walked her to the door and watched jealously, as the same man each evening, waited outside the gate for Barbra.

When Stefan returned to his father, Alexie was back from his chat with the carriage driver and was again seated at the table.

"Marry her!" said his father once more, of course, meaning Barbra.

Ignoring his father's remark, Stefan asked Alexie, "How early are you leaving in the morning?"

"I have been speaking with the driver who I know well, he has worked for us a long time." said Alexie. "He wants to sleep in the barn. I told him we had room for him here, but he wants to be with the horses. To answer your question, I think we will leave early, perhaps at daybreak."

Stefan sat next to his father, across from Alexie. "I will miss you, Alexie. I have so enjoyed your company." he said.

"I need to be with Sofie, but I will miss you, too." said Alexie. "Seeing what has happened here, in just a few days, has been exciting."

Stefan saw the slivovica and poured himself a glass, offering some to Alexie. "It will seem odd, being here alone." said Stefan.

"You aren't alone. You have Pas." Looking around, Alexie said, "Where is Pas?"

"I saw Ignatz take him out." said Anton. Then, after a long pause, Anton said, "If you don't mind, I would like to stay awhile."

Stefan's face lit with pleasure. "Oh, Ta...can you be gone from Vladezemla so long? I would love to have you stay here." Then he quickly added, "I must warn you, Ignatz does not cook, so we eat out often."

Anton smiled, "I would like that very much."

Later that evening, the three men took a stroll to Strassmayerov where the Palace Hotel was located. On the way, they passed women selling small bunches of violets tied with string.

Inside the elegant dining room at the Palace Hotel, the three were seated at a round table covered with a white cloth. On the center was a small vase with purple perunika. The perunika is a variety of Iris, its name derived from Perun, a god of Slavic mythology.

A waiter wearing black pants, white shirt and a spotless white apron greeted them. "Dobar vecher...Good evening." he said, handing them each a menu.

After studying the menu, they unanimously decided on janjetina s krumpirom, lamb with potatoes and they had good Croatian wine with their meal. The service was excellent and the men were greatly enjoying themselves, putting aside for now, the worries about Katya, Ivan and Alexie's journey to Trieste. With their after dinner coffee and brandy, they indulged in strong Turkish cigarettes.

Stefan's eyes grew wide as he saw approaching their table, the man who waited for Barbra each evening. He was a handsome older man. His perfectly trimmed salt and pepper hair framed his unlined face. He had a nice straight nose, clear grey green eyes. He gave the appearance of an educated and cultured man.

In halting Croatian, the man tried to introduce himself, but he didn't have a good command of the language. All three men rose from their seats. Anton, realizing the man could not speak Croatian well, spoke to him in German, while the very surprised Alexie and Stefan stared. Stefan had no idea his father was fluent in the German language, which had been mandatory when Anton was in school. Stefan and Alexie stood dumbly, while Anton and the man conversed. The man shook hands with Anton, bowed politely to Alexie and Stefan and walked towards the table where they could see Barbra sipping what looked like an aperitif.

"You speak German?" said a surprised Stefan as they all sat down. "What did he want?" All sorts of thoughts raced through Stefan's mind. *Was this man supporting Barbra? Did he want her to quit working for Stefan? Were they leaving?*

"I am having lunch with him tomorrow. There are things he wants to discuss...to clarify." said Anton, trying to hide a smile that was playing on his lips.

"Discuss what...clarify what?" Stefan was sure that this man was going take Barbra away. "Who is he?" insisted Stefan, his mind in a whirl. *My Tata speaks German and I didn't know that!*

Stefan asked again, "Who is he?"

With a broad smile, Anton said, "Das ist der Papa...her father."

CHAPTER 29

Alexie, anxious to leave for Trieste, was dressed and ready before daylight. He knocked at each of their doors, letting them know he was leaving. Wearing only dressing gowns, father and son followed Alexie downstairs. After hugs and handshakes, Alexie was on his way.

Stefan and Anton in their robes, sat at their usual table in the back, where Ignatz had already placed hot coffee and savijaca od sira...cheese strudel.

Seeing Pas staring at the table, Ignatz advised, "You shouldn't give him any strudel. He ate the other one whole just a few minutes ago."

With a stern look, Stefan waved his hand and said, "Odi." With a sigh and what sounded like a grumble, the huge dog ambled to the foot of the stairs, where he lay down staring at them.

Stefan cut a slice of the cheese strudel. As if he were thinking out loud, he said, "I almost feel guilty."

Anton turned and looked at him. "And, why is that?" he asked.

He put his strudel on a small plate. "Because," he answered hesitantly, "because, Ivan and Katya have so many problems and I feel very happy." He continued, "It doesn't seem right that things are going so well for me and so badly for them."

"Be grateful." said his father, stirring sugar in his coffee. "We each have our own Destiny and we do the best that we can with what we are given or with what we lose."

They ate in silence, each lost in their own thoughts. When they were finished, Anton said, "I have been doing a lot of thinking...thinking about my life and I want to know your reaction to my plan."

"What plan?" asked Stefan, interested.

Anton proceeded cautiously, "If what I propose does not suit you, I will understand and not be offended."

"What is it, Ta?" Stefan was starting to worry.

Anton watched Stefan's face as he spoke, "I believe I would like to live in Zagreb." Seeing the surprised look on Stefan's face he went on, "I don't think I want to live at Vladezemla anymore."

Stefan was more surprised than concerned, "Can you leave? Ivan is no longer there, who will be in charge?"

Before answering the questions, Anton asked, "Just tell me…am I welcome in this house? Will you be uncomfortable if I stay here?"

"Oh, Ta! It would be wonderful if you stayed here." Stefan was so pleased. "I thought you loved Vladezemla too much to ever leave. It was all that you talked about when I was at home. But, who will take care of it now that Ivan is gone?"

"Oh, Stefan…" Anton didn't realize he would be so moved. His throat tightened with emotion. He took a moment to compose himself. "I was fearful you wouldn't want your father about, that I might be in your way."

Again Stefan said, "I want you here, but you haven't told me how you can leave Vladezemla."

Before he could go on, Anton needed wine to calm him. He reached for the wine which was always at the side table. He poured a glass for himself and one for Stefan.

"I have thought much about this." He began. "Vera wanted Vladezemla for Ivan because she resented my arranged marriage to your mother. When I was a student here, I fell in love with Vera and I suppose we talked of a future together." Anton took a sip of wine. "I hung onto the land for you and Ivan. You have made a life for yourself, one of success and excitement. Ivan is gone and he may never return."

Stefan said nothing, just reached across the table and patted his father's hand affectionately.

Anton smiled at his son and went on, "I won't sell the land. It is still for you and Ivan. I was thinking that Marko and Vera could move into the house with Klara and take care of things."

"Would Marko do that?" asked Stefan.

"If he doesn't want to, I know Vera will. She will move there herself and he will have to follow." Anton laughed at the picture in his mind of Vera dragging her possessions up the hill alone.

146

He said, "I trust Marko more than any other man I know. He is a good man and I love him like a brother. He is smart and he will know how to handle the men and keep things in order."

Thinking out loud, Anton said, "I could possibly go back once a month or so, to go over the accounts. Marko and I will work out some sort of financial arrangement that will suit him...and Vera."

Later, nearing lunchtime, a nicely dressed Anton was strolling about the main floor, looking at the items for sale, noticing that not many had prices on them. It appeared that Barbra was also a negotiator, pricing items when she saw who was interested in a purchase.

After seeing how Lucia, in Trieste, was surrounded with beautiful things from around the world, Anton was sure he, too, could enjoy surrounding himself with such treasures.

Barbra and Stefan were in the office going through some jewelry traded for a cloisonné vase. Anton had tried speaking to Barbra in German, but she preferred to use and perfect her grasp of the Croatian language.

Barbra heard the door open. Expecting her father she hurried to greet him. They spoke in hushed tones and it appeared that Barbra was trying to give her father instructions, which he halted with a stern look.

The two fathers, each ignoring their offspring, shook hands and casually walked out into the beautiful summer day.

Both men looked elegant, Anton in a grey suit and Herr Pressler in a dark blue suit with a matching derby hat. Anton didn't have a hat, but thought he just might have to try a derby and see if it suited him.

Seated at an outdoor table near the square, the two men, very comfortable with one another, ate a tomato salad, sausages and potatoes, good crusty bread and drank wine.

Both men, smoking their after lunch cigarettes, continued with their important luncheon conversation.

"So, Karl," said Anton, now both on a first name basis. "When do you think your sister will arrive?"

"She sent word that by train it will take her three days. But, she didn't tell me when she was leaving Germany." Karl waved for the waiter to come, "Bring me some fresh water." The waiter understood and nodded.

Karl thanked the waiter when he brought the water with a nod and said to Anton, "I will stay with Barbra until my sister arrives. Barbra insists on staying to work for your son, but of course it isn't proper for her to be here alone."

"Of course." agreed Anton. "We have rooms upstairs above the gallery. Your sister and Barbra are welcome to stay there instead of a hotel. They will be our welcomed guests."

Karl Pressler felt confident leaving his daughter in Zagreb. He and Barbra had several discussions about her returning home, all of them ending with Barbra in tears. Now, that he had met Anton, he was sure with his sister as chaperone and with Anton as a respectable older man, Barbra would be properly treated and well looked after.

The two fathers returned to the shop, arm in arm, laughing over something they both found amusing. Stefan had no clue what purpose the lunch had, if any, but Barbra knew. She watched as the men entered. She went directly to her father, with no polite greetings, and pulled him aside for a private conversation.

Stefan alongside his father asked, "What do you suppose that is about?"

Anton, once again, trying to hide a smile said, "I think it has to do with Barbra going home or staying here."

Stefan's heart sank. "He is taking her home? Oh, Ta, he can't do that!"

It was evident that Barbra and her father were disagreeing on something. Barbra with arms crossed over her chest, plopped herself in a chair with all the pouting of a ten year old child. Her father made some parting remark to his daughter, looked over to where Anton and Stefan stood, tipped his hat, smiled and strolled out the open door.

Stefan started to hurry to Barbra's side, but Anton grabbed his arm. "Don't worry," he said. "We have made arrangements...she is staying."

Barbra stood up. Looked up to heaven sighed deeply and walked towards them.

Stefan went to her, "Are you alright?" he asked.

"No…" she said, in a low controlled voice, "My Tante Gerta is coming to stay with me as my chaperone."

CHAPTER 30

In Trieste, Katya was a very happy young woman. She and Lucia, her Nona, walked to the market near the bay and shopped for fresh flowers, fruit, and fish. It was as it had been before, she and Lucia were having a great time. Katya still made faces when she saw the baskets of wriggling eels or the tables with the tiny sparrow-sized dead birds for sale...a delicacy she couldn't bring herself to try.

Lucia shaded herself with a black lace umbrella, while Katya wore a wide-brimmed hat trimmed with a yellow ribbon matching her yellow full skirted dress. The swelling from her attack was almost all gone and the exposure of the sun on her face, gave her enough color to hide the already fading bruises.

She carried a large straw bag in which she put their purchases. Not far from the dock were tables under a blue and white awning. Here the two always had a delicious limonada, where the lemon juice was freshly squeezed when the drink was ordered.

Looking out at the harbor, Katya jumped up shouting, "Look, Nona. It is the Vincenti. She is coming home." The ship owned by the Renaldi Import Company was returning from its trip to Greece and Turkey with merchandise to be sold to vendors and sent throughout Italy.

Katya was excited. "I am going tomorrow to help with the unpacking. I can't wait to see what is there."

Lucia smiled remembering how long ago as a girl, she was just this excited when the ship would return with exotic looking masks from Africa or rugs from Turkey and painted pottery from Greece. Lucia's mother cried and argued that the warehouse and the shipping docks were no place for a refined young woman, but Lucia didn't care what her mother thought, for Lucia loved the ships, the sea, and most of all, her father.

"Come, my Piccolina...my little one, time to go home." said Lucia affectionately, watching her precious Katya jumping up and down with excitement at seeing the ship floating closer to the harbor.

Katya took Lucia's arm and the two walked slowly through the marketplace to the road leading up the hill to their house. Katya thought she saw Zolton, but it was just another Gypsy. Disappointed, she looked away.

It was close to noon and soon all the banks and businesses would be closed for the Italian siesta. The streets were deserted from noon to two o'clock a tradition going back to the Romans. Everyone takes a nap after lunch.

At the hilltop house, Ivan had trouble falling asleep during the day. Instead of napping, he would go to the terrace and sit near the wall enjoying the sun. The house was very quiet. Today he pulled a letter from his pocket, a letter from his father Anton. It had been delivered early that morning, but until now he didn't have the time to read it. His work at the import company kept him busy all morning.

Like Katya, he enjoyed seeing the items from all the faraway places. His job was to keep track of the inventory. He found it to be easy and interesting work. Ruda was pleasant enough to work for and now, with Alexie back it was even more enjoyable, for Alexie was teaching him different aspects of the business.

To his surprise, he found he could be comfortable around Katya. She behaved towards him as she always had. She never mentioned the Gypsies, not even Queen Valina. Ivan was hoping she would in time forget Zolton.

A slight breeze rustled the letter in his hand bringing his attention back to it. It was the first letter from Anton since Alexie's return a week ago. Alexie had told them all about Stefan's house and business, the Vladeslav Kolekcija, about the beautiful art seller, Barbra, and how much Stefan loved Zagreb and even possibly loved Barbra.

Ivan opened the letter and as he read, he couldn't believe what was written there. He wanted to wake everyone in the house and share it with them. He kept reading, almost disbelieving the words. How was it that his other father, Marko was now in charge of Vladezemla? His mother, Vera, is living in the house where Ernesta Vladeslav lived? Anton now lives in Zagreb with Stefan and is working on restoring Magda's old house. Vladezemla has been equally deeded over to Ivan and Stefan. Now the art seller, Barbra is living in the house with Stefan, Anton and her Tante Gerta.

He continued reading about how much Anton loved being in Zagreb, the excitement, the people and so on. It was as if he had never known his father-godfather at all! "Boze Moy...My God." he said, using Klara's favorite phrase.

Ivan was able to find some writing paper in a credenza on the main floor. It pleased him that he didn't have to climb the stairs searching for writing paper. He wanted to reply to the letter he had just finished reading. He had so many questions. It all sounded so very exciting. He wanted to ask if he could visit Zagreb. Surely it would be safe. Ivan was anxious to see everything first described by Alexie upon his arrival to Trieste and then all he read in Anton's letter. He was especially anxious to see Stefan, now that they were real brothers with all the past unhappiness behind them.

Ivan didn't have any stamps, so he wanted to get to the post office as soon as it opened. From the post office, it was only a short walk to the Renaldi warehouse.

The lightweight walking stick Klara found for him at Vladezemla had been replaced by a sturdy wooden cane. The new cane was strong and gave him the support he needed when walking.

Mia was coming to the terrace to water plants as Ivan was leaving.

"Tell Alexie I am going to the post office then I will walk to the warehouse." he said.

She nodded and went about the business of watering the plants. Mia moved to the plants at the wall overlooking the road which meandered downhill. Lucia's house was the last on the hill, so it was a seldom used road, except for friends or deliveries. Mia saw a group of young dark skinned men were bouncing and tossing a large ball to one another. She wondered what Gypsies were doing up here, so near the house.

The men were tossing the ball and running very near Ivan as he walked down the hill, almost bumping into him. The reckless manner in which they were running on the road and tossing the ball triggered a warning in Mia. She screamed out, "Ivan..." just as one of the men gave Ivan a shove, sending him down the stone hillside to the beach below.

Mia, now screaming hysterically ran into the house calling for Alexie, who having completed his nap, was already on his way down the stairs. Bewildered, he followed the screaming Mia as she ran down the road to the spot where Ivan was pushed over the wall.

The road was deserted. The only evidence was the large ball caught in a bush.

Katya hearing the scream was next, running right behind Alexie. When she saw Ivan lying on the beach below, she screamed so loudly it woke up the still napping Sofie and Lucia. Alexie and Katya ran as fast as they could down the gravel road, leaping over a small wall when they reached the beach. Mia stood in the road screaming for help and for the polizia.

Katya felt a wave of nausea and thought she was going to be sick when she saw Ivan. He was bruised and unconscious, just as he had been long ago when he had been struck and tumbled down the hill on the night the Turk was killed.

This couldn't be happening again!

Alexie was kneeling next to Ivan. He shouted excitedly, "He is alive. He's breathing."

The polizia arrived and held back the curious crowd. Feeling sick, Katya forced herself to kneel next to Alexie. Carefully she took Ivan's hand. She felt his fingers and moved her hands tenderly up his arm, searching for breaks.

"We have to get him to a hospital." said Alexie.

Katya caught the sight of a woman in the crowd behind Alexie. The woman wasn't dressed like a Gypsy, but her skin and hair were dark like most of the Gypsy woman Katya had known. Her smile was menacing sending a chill through Katya.

"No...not the hospital." said Katya, "We can't risk it. The Gypsies did this. They are here!" Katya pointed to where the woman stood, but the woman was gone.

Mia was at their side. "Katya is right." She said, "I saw the young men who did this, they could have been Gypsies."

Katya turned to Mia, "Mia, tell the polizia that we are taking him home. Not the hospital. And, tell them we need help carrying him."

The young policeman argued with Mia saying Ivan should be taken to the hospital. Mia told the young policeman that he might get into trouble if he defied Seniora Lucia Kurecka, whose nephew this was.

Ivan was hand-carried on a makeshift stretcher by Alexie and a young strong fisherman.

Sofie and Lucia were waiting in front of the house watching an unconscious Ivan being carried up the road with Mia running ahead of them.

Once in the house, Mia ran into a storage room and alone, dragged out a mattress which she placed on the middle of the floor.

Afraid of further hurting Ivan by moving him, the stretcher with him still on it, was placed on the mattress.

Lucia pressed some lire in the fisherman's hand as thanks for helping carry Ivan. He tried to refuse, but she insisted, sending him away with a grateful smile.

Mia appeared with a pan of water, some antiseptic, gauze, cotton and anything else that she felt would be helpful.

Sofie was crying softly. She was frightened, fearful Ivan wouldn't make it this time.

Katya kneeled on the floor and lowered her ear to hear Ivan's heartbeat. She heard it, but wasn't sure if it was too slow, but she was glad she heard it.

Just as she and the young Luba had done two years earlier in Vladezemla, now Mia and Katya gently removed Ivan's clothing by cutting the cloth, trying not to hurt him.

Dear God, she silently prayed, *I did this. This is my fault. The Gypsies are here because of me.*

The young uniformed policeman followed them into the house, saying he needed to report the incident. He was young, smooth skinned, nice looking with dark eyes and dark hair.

Alexie, concerned for how this would play out if it were known that Gypsies had attacked Ivan, walked out with the young carbinieri. Alexie led the man down the road on the pretense of examining where the accident took place. Finding Ivan's cane Alexie alleged that Ivan being crippled had lost his footing and fell. The lawyer in Alexie took over and he spoke as if presenting a case thoroughly fabricating how Ivan must have fallen.

Satisfied with Alexie's version of the accident, the policeman left. Returning to the house, an excited Alexie said, "He may not be hurt as bad as we think. I looked over the wall where he fell. It was a smooth wall of rock. Hopefully he only slid down without breaking anything."

Ivan, wearing only underpants had every part of his body gently touched and examined. He had a bump on his forehead, not nearly as bad as any Katya had sported when she was attacked with the rocks. His left arm and the left side of his body showed scrapes with some minor bleeding.

"Katya pointed to the scratches, "He must have slid on his left side."

Mia was holding a cold damp towel on Ivan's head.

Lucia, just as Klara would, had a rosary in her hand. She sat in a plush chair nearby softly sobbing, while Sofie sat on the sofa, her face stained with tears.

Lucia said, "We must call a doctor. He may have hurt something inside."

Alexie said, "Yes, we should call a doctor, but I am confident that there is no real bad damage to his body. It is lucky that the wall was only about three feet high where he went over. And," he went on, "it doesn't appear he dropped, but slid. His clothes helped protect his body during the slide."

The doctor came, suggested Ivan be taken to the hospital as a precautionary measure, but had to admit he didn't think the fall was as grave as it could have been. He left some pills for the pain and some awful smelling salve for the swelling bruises, which Katya planned to replace with an herbal salve of her own.

Sofie didn't leave the couch, but Lucia went upstairs to her room. Just as she had prayed for her Vincent so long ago, she once more dropped a pillow at the side of her bed, kneeled and now said the rosary for Ivan.

Alexie kept vigil, dozing fitfully in one of the chairs alongside the sofa, with his shirt tail out and his collar button undone.

Katya lay on the floor on a blanket next to the mattress where Ivan lay. His body covered only with a lightweight blanket. She didn't think she slept, but must have dozed, because she awoke whenever she heard him moan.

When it was morning, the sunlight streamed through the glass terrace doors onto Katya's sleeping face. She opened her eyes and instantly turned to look at Ivan. His open eyes were staring at her.

"Am I alright?" he asked, "What happened?"

Katya sat up and felt his forehead. No fever, a good sign. She said, "You fell over the wall and down the side of the hill." She said nothing about his being pushed. Better to wait until he was stronger.

Seeing the concern in her eyes, Ivan smiled and said, "Haven't we done this before?"

Hearing the conversation Sofie said, "Thank God, Hvala Bog, you are awake."

Alexie freshly dressed and planning to go to the warehouse went directly to Ivan. He knelt down and studied his face. "You look better." he announced, relieved. He turned and gave Sofie a kiss and said, "He looks better doesn't he?"

With goose down pillows and several blankets, Ivan still on the floor, was maneuvered into a sitting position. To his own and everyone else's surprise, it wasn't as painful a move as anticipated. His left side ached and the bump on his forehead hurt when touched, but he knew that he was feeling much better than after the fall two years ago in Vladezemla.

Katya and Mia hovered over Ivan. Sofie never left the sofa, wishing she could do something more for Ivan than just worry.

Lucia didn't dress today. She wore a colorful caftan from one of their Trinidad shipments. No one but the family ever saw her in the caftans and it was the only departure from the widow's black she allowed herself.

With a cup of cappuccino in her hand, she strolled about the terrace, deep in thought. *Thank God, Ivan would be alright soon. Would the Gypsies come back?* She was worried.

The warm morning sun felt wonderful to Lucia. The terrace wall was high so that it was private. She would suggest that Ivan be brought out in the fresh air and sunlight. It would be good for him.

On his walk to the warehouse, down the road and across the harbor plaza, Alexie wondered if he was being followed. He didn't turn to look back, but kept walking only stopping at a shop window now and then, checking the reflection to see if someone was behind him.

At the warehouse he greeted the men stacking bales and boxes of merchandise. Before going through the doorway, Alexie paused and looked back. He saw no one, but Alexie felt he was being watched.

A cot was placed on the terrace. With the help of Lucia's man servant Julian, Ivan got to his feet. Surprising himself and everyone watching, Ivan slowly with some discomfort, made it out to the terrace.

Once on the cot, still wearing only underpants covered by a towel, he lay in the healing sunlight, somewhat confused as to how he had fallen, for no one mentioned the Gypsies.

Katya went upstairs to freshen up and change her clothes. Sofie on the terrace, still in her nightgown sat in a chair at the table to be near Ivan, while Lucia in her colorful caftan, patrolled the terrace like a soldier.

Hearing the iron door knocker sounding, Lucia went to the terrace entry where she could watch Mia answer the knock.

She couldn't make out what Mia was saying, but could tell that Mia was arguing and refusing the person at the door. Lucia saw Mia close the door and to Lucia's surprise, Mia bolted the door.

When Lucia came into the room, Mia seeing her said, "A Gypsy woman wanting to come in. She said she had lace and rings to sell."

Lucia's heart sank. This wasn't good. Never had they had a Gypsy…ever…come to the door to sell something. When the Gypsies were in Trieste, they would set up a table or stall in the market place.

Lucia said, "Send Julian to the warehouse. We need Alexie, now!"

Alexie, along with Ruda came as soon as they could. Alexie filled Ruda in on what had happened. There was no keeping Ruda at the warehouse, when there might be danger or a fight. Alexie watched for Gypsies as they hurried to the house, but saw none.

Mia with the door bolted watched for Alexie from an upper window. She hurried down and unlocked the door when the men arrived.

"They are on the terrace." she told them, the worry evident in her voice.

Alexie with Ruda behind him hurried to the terrace.

The two men saw Sofie seated at the table, Ivan was on the cot, while Lucia and Katya were nervously pacing.

Lucia announced, "A Gypsy came to the door pretending to sell something, she wanted to come in. Mia wouldn't let her in." Then she added, "In all the years I have been here, no Gypsy has ever tried to sell me something at the door."

A confused Ivan asked, "What is going on?"

Alexie said, "You didn't fall over the wall. You were pushed by some Gypsy boys."

Even with the red bump on his forehead and the darkening bruising, Ivan's face went white. He said softly, "Valina was right. They want revenge."

Lucia said, "I will get dressed. I will go in town and I will search for Valina and plead with her."

"No…it will do no good." said, Katya.

Feeling defeated she sat down. "Valina said she could not help us. My bracelet won't protect me this time."

Ruda offered a cigarette to Ivan lying on the cot. No one spoke for a moment.

"We have to get them out of here." said Ruda. "We have to send them away."

Sofie sobbed, "Oh God, no…"

Lucia called to Mia, "Send Julian for the priest…the young one. Tell him to bring his prayer book."

As if sharing one mind, Ruda and Lucia nodded to one another in agreement.

The others just stared at them confused. Alexie asked, "What are you thinking?"

After a pause, Lucia said, "The priest will marry them."

Ruda said, "The Vincenti will take them away from Trieste."

Ivan and Katya looked at each other more than a little surprised. Hesitating, Ivan asked Katya, "Do you want to marry me? I mean, would you marry me?"

Katya looked at Ivan, lying on the cot, his body damaged because of her actions. It was her fault he was attacked. She said what she thought was the right thing to say.

"Yes," she said, softly. "I will marry you."

Alexie took Katya's hand and also Ivan's. Alexie knew about Zolton. Knowing the story he only said, "You two must take care of one other. You will be away from family and friends. You will only have each other."

At the table, Sofie dropped her head on her crossed arms and sobbed. Her heart was breaking. Destiny was denying her both Katya and Ivan…cruel Destiny!

When the slender, blond-haired, boyish-faced Father Pietro arrived, he thought he was summoned to perform the last rites. Why else would he be asked to hurry and bring his prayer book?

Pietro was taken aback when he saw Lucia in the bright caftan for he had never seen her in anything but black.

The scene he witnessed on the terrace was bizarre to say the least. A woman in her nightgown was at the table sobbing hysterically; a nearly naked man was lying on a cot; a tough little man's stare was making him uncomfortable and a servant was bringing out a large candle, wine and wine glasses.

The man on the cot didn't look as though he needed the last rites.

Seeing the puzzled look on the young priest's face, Lucia said, "We want you to perform a marriage."

"A what?" The young priest was stunned. "A marriage... impossible!"

"I want you to marry my granddaughter and the young man on the cot." said Lucia.

"I can't do that." The priest stammered. "We need to post bans...and...this is not a church." He looked at all the faces staring at him. "This isn't proper. You can't ask me to do this."

"I am asking and you will do it." said Lucia softly.

"It is a sin." he protested.

"It will be my sin." said Lucia, "We are forcing you to do this." And she added, "Need I remind you who paid for the repairs to the broken stained glass windows."

The young priest was shocked. "You are bribing me and...I think you are threatening me."

Ruda got into the frightened priest's face. "I think you should marry them." His voice was menacing.

With a quavering voice, the priest said, "The bishop will hear of this. It is an outrage."

Lucia said, calmly, "Tell the bishop he is welcome here, anytime."

She slipped her own wedding ring from her finger and handed it to Katya.

Young Father Pietro visibly upset, with his prayer book shaking in his hands, performed a marriage ceremony in the open air on a terrace, uniting an almost naked man lying on a cot to a beautiful girl wearing a bracelet adorned with pagan symbols.

When the ceremony was completed, everyone shook the priest's hand, filled his pockets with lire, thanked him profusely and sent the bewildered young man on his way.

Mia filled the wine glasses and everyone toasted Katya and Ivan, who were both feeling embarrassed, aware that their marriage was only a necessary arrangement.

Ruda said, "Well and good. They are married. The scared priest did not have a marriage certificate. And…we do not have passports or documents." He was looking directly at Alexie when he said this.

Alexie said, "We will buy them tomorrow. Passports are no problem."

Ruda said, thinking out loud, "I can have the ship ready to travel in couple of days."

Katya sipped her wine. Looking at Lucia, her grandmother, she asked, "Where will we go?"

With a broad smile, Lucia said, "To Amerika, my Piccolina…to Amerika!"

Ivan and Katya looked on bewildered, as all the others raised their glasses and toasted in unison, "TO AMERIKA!"

THE END

Karma rewarded and punished, while Destiny Denied.

EPILOGUE

In time, to Anton's delight, Stefan married the beautiful and very smart Barbra Pressler. Tante Gerta, Barbra's aunt and Anton became great friends and companions.

Ignatz accepted the invasion of women with grace and even allowed part of his living quarters to be used as a kitchen. Gerta prepared German meals of Sauerbraten, Wienerschnitzel, Spaetzel, and German Potato Salad to everyone's pleasure, especially Pas, who enjoyed the leftovers.

At last, Vera was mistress of Vladezemla. Twenty years earlier at Anton and Ernesta's engagement party the pregnant Vera had been turned away from the kitchen door. Now, with Ivan gone and only Marko and Klara as companions, being in the house was not what she had dreamed and hoped for.

Sofie gave birth to a baby boy in March. The baby's arrival took away some of the pain left by the departure of Ivan and Katya. He was named Aleksy after his father, but with the spelling used by Lucia Kurecka's husband.

For the first time after twenty years, the Gypsies did not return to Vladezemla to Marko Balaban's land during their annual trip to France. Nor would they ever return. They were missed by the villagers for the arrival of the Gypsies meant a festival of music and dancing and trading.

For the rest of her life, Lucia watched the road from her Trieste terrace, hoping for the arrival of her dear friend, Queen Valina, who never came.

CPSIA information can be obtained at www.ICGtesting.com
Printed in the USA
BVOW031740140113

310580BV00002B/5/P